**What was th[...]
no, she was [...]n!**

Hannah jumped [...] [...]rd the kitchen.

Tyrel was already stomping the last sparks from a dishcloth and running water into her egg pan. "What the devil!" he roared, then gaped as he saw her.

Hannah willed herself not to blush. "I was coming to put out the fire," she said.

"Yeah." He eyed her. Slowly. Thoughtfully. "You could have beat it out with the towel. Course then you'd'a been naked. You *are* naked under there, aren't you?"

She was silent for a moment. "You, Mr. Fox, have the mind of an adolescent goat."

"And you, Miss Nelson, have really nice..." His gaze skimmed her body, her long, elegant throat, the high rise of her breasts, the endless length of her tanned legs. "Diction."

Dear Reader,

Summer brings such pleasant images to mind, ice cream and a day at the beach...great-looking men glistening with suntan lotion...oops! I need to pull my mind back to the topic of Love & Laughter. Nevertheless, in this month's selection, we do have two hunky and adorable heroes to raise your temperatures.

Big, bad boy toy Tony Russo is a lot sexier and much more delicious than Lynn Morgan ever imagined. Lynn convinced her straitlaced lawyer buddy, Tony Russo, to play the role of her no-good boyfriend. More *GQ* than bad-boy material, Lynn feared he couldn't pull it off. But when she saw him transformed into black leather and attitude, she all but forgot about her little scheme. All she could think about was taking a walk on the wild side...in *Operation Gigolo* by Vicki Lewis Thompson.

The last thing pampered rich girl Hannah Nelson wants is a cowboy, but when she's forced to hide out at the Lone Oak Ranch, she begins to see Tyrel Fox in a very different light! The swaggering, sexy cowboy was just so...so elemental, Hannah decided. But would he be more than a change of pace? Find out in *Counterfeit Cowgirl* by Lois Greiman.

Enjoy the summer heat!

Malle Vallik

Malle Vallik
Associate Senior Editor

COUNTERFEIT COWGIRL
Lois Greiman

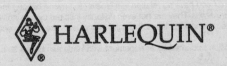

HARLEQUIN®

TORONTO • NEW YORK • LONDON
AMSTERDAM • PARIS • SYDNEY • HAMBURG
STOCKHOLM • ATHENS • TOKYO • MILAN • MADRID
PRAGUE • WARSAW • BUDAPEST • AUCKLAND

ISBN 0-373-44048-0

COUNTERFEIT COWGIRL

A funny thing happened...

While growing up on a North Dakota wheat farm, I acquired lots of sophisticated talents—pitching manure, stacking hay and turning unborn calves. Those talents stood me in good stead during the years I spent as a horse trainer, but I didn't expect them to come in handy once I began writing romance fiction. Strangely enough, they have.

Counterfeit Cowgirl gave me the chance to relive the beauty of a frosty morning spent in the cattle yards, to remember the miracle of welcoming a newborn calf into the world—and I didn't even have to freeze my fingers to experience it. Writing it was as much fun as I can have with my boots on. But what the heck, *you* might as well live dangerously—take off your boots and read it in bed!

—Lois Greiman

To Gary Nelson, who long ago declared me half horse and half Indian, and who taught me the fine art of blowing my nose without a handkerchief.

1

IT WAS SNOWING IN HELL!

Squinting through the cracked windshield of her '82 Rabbit, Hannah tried to read the nearest road sign. The words *Valley Green* were still discernible, but the rest of the letters were obliterated by the swirling, blinding snow. It was congealing on her windshield wipers like clotted cream, but she refused to knock off the frozen globs one more time.

She hated this sad excuse of a car, she hated this state, and she *hated* being Hannah Nelson.

This couldn't be happening to her. It was all a nightmare.

No civilized being lived in North Dakota. She'd refused to come here, of course. But raving hadn't worked. She'd switched to cajoling, but even then Daddy had remained uncharacteristically stubborn.

A slit of road became visible through the swirling snow. Hannah slammed on the brakes. Her car careened sideways, then slid dangerously toward a ditch. Her heart thumped in her chest. Please, God, don't let her die. Not here, a thousand miles from the nearest Macy's. The Rabbit's bald tires finally grabbed hold and came to a jarring halt facing the crossroad. So this must be it—the road to The Lone Oak Ranch, the final leg of her journey into hell.

Frowning, Hannah stared back down the highway. Long fingers of snowdrifts slanted across the tar road behind her. She shivered, wishing with all her soul she could simply turn around and return home.

After all, none of this was her fault. None of it! Still, perhaps it wouldn't kill her to apologize.

If a lady lost her pride, she lost everything, her mother had said. And no one with any pride would apologize to a man who called himself Lucky Lindy. Even if she *had* called him a fat toad. Even if he was associated with men who called themselves Eddie the Knife and Mugsy Two Toes. Even if her life was in danger of being snuffed out by a couple of goons whose boss she'd insulted.

Fighting back tears, Hannah tightened her grip on the steering wheel, depressed the accelerator and...the engine killed.

Frustration roared up inside her. But there was no one around to blame, and no one to impress with her tears, though she had perfected the art of crying without smudging her makeup. So there was nothing to do but start the car and continue on. She turned the key. The engine coughed wearily and fell silent.

A degree of fear began to replace Hannah's frustration. A person could freeze to death in a matter of minutes out here, couldn't she?

Calming her nerves, Hannah tried the key again. The engine turned over, chugged, and miraculously started.

The gravel road was slippery and hard to see, but Daddy said The Lone Oak would be impossible to miss. It was a large, lucrative ranch. State of the art.

She crested a hill and began to descend. Her wipers scraped against the windshield, echoing the headache that had begun several hours before.

Through a narrow arc of clear glass, she caught sight of a driveway on her left, but no massive house or impressive barns could be seen. She drove on, leaning over the steering wheel in an attempt to see through the blizzard. Still she saw nothing but arctic white and the tops of a few fence posts leaning dismally into the driving snow.

Finally, certain she had somehow missed her turn, Hannah stopped the Rabbit to read her directions once more. But the instructions remained the same.

Turning her car around was tricky, but she managed it with only slight heart palpitations. After a few miles, the lone driveway appeared again, on her right this time. She squinted through the storm, and thought she saw a house at the end of the lane.

There was little else to do but turn in and ask for new directions. The house was an old two-story, sided by narrow slats and partially covered by peeling white paint. She pulled to a stop in front of it.

When she stepped from the car a gust of wind knocked her back a pace. Slush seeped into the fine suede of her newly purchased half boots—the perfect attire for a romp in the country and a bargain at $499, the salesclerk had said.

Hannah scowled down at them, lifted one from the mire, then caught a glimpse of a man through the swirling snow. Lowering her foot with a soggy splash, Hannah watched him approach. The brim of his felt Australian hat was turned down in front. In his arms was a calf, a slimy calf, nestled like his own kin against his frayed denim jacket and worn jeans.

"So you got here, then?" he said, stopping for an instant before stepping around her to climb the stairs of the slanted porch. "Been expecting you. Can you get the door?"

"What?" Hannah asked, staring after him in bewilderment.

He motioned toward the door with his head, jostling the calf he carried. "The door."

So the natives were slow, Hannah thought, and found she was not the least bit surprised. Deepening her scowl, she followed his slushy footsteps to the porch and up. "I can only assume you realize you have a calf in your arms," she said.

The cowboy glanced down at the newborn as if surprised to see it, then raised his gaze to hers. "Dad said you was bright."

Hannah stared at him for a moment. She'd been on the road for four days. Her head hurt, her teeth had sprouted moss, and she hated men who thought themselves amusing. Especially when they were sadly mistaken.

She raised one brow at him. "I believe you're under the false impression that you know me, sir."

"You came here for a job, right?" he said, fumbling around the calf to open the door himself.

She smiled, knowing just the corners of her mouth would curl upward. It was an expression she reserved for peasants and oafs. This man was obviously both. "I'm afraid not. I simply stopped by for directions."

The cowboy stepped inside. The calf's rubbery hooves banged against the doorjamb.

"Come on in. Close the door."

She dropped the smile. "I told you, I just stopped for directions. It seems I'm lost."

"No, you're not. I found you." He laid the calf on the cracked linoleum of the cluttered living room. A guitar was nestled against a dying jade. Setting aside his hat, he straightened with a grin that creased twin dimples into his lean cheeks. "Come on in. We'll hunker down by the fire and dream about Jamaica."

Hannah straightened her back to ramrod stiffness and pursed her lips. She'd been courted by millionaires and celebrities. Not one of them had gotten so much as an invitation to dinner. This cowboy's two-bit charm was unlikely to impress her, even though he had Robert Redford's disarming smile and the Marlboro man's chiseled jaw.

"Thanks so for your kind offer," she said with ringing insincerity. "But as tempting as it sounds, I'm afraid I'm not the...hunkering type. I simply need directions, Mr...."

"Fox." The cowboy stepped forward, offering his hand in greeting. "Tyrel Fox."

"Tyrel..." Hannah echoed. She suddenly felt sick to her stomach. "This is not..." She shook her head and motioned vaguely toward her surroundings. "This isn't The Lone Oak Ranch."

"'Fraid you're mistaken," he said, and nodded toward the barn.

Hannah turned to stare in that direction, then squinted at a sign hung above the broad double doors. The words *The Lone*

Oak could be seen even through the driving snow. She turned back in a daze.

"This is the Oak, and I'm Ty," he said, and, catching her hand, shook it firmly.

Hers immediately felt sticky. She ended the greeting abruptly, pulling her fingers from his grip and grimacing at the filth he'd left behind.

"You must be Hannah Nelson. I'm glad to see you," he said, seeming oblivious to her horror as he watched her face. "You just made me ten bucks."

"I've no idea what you're talking about," she said.

"Me, I'm not the betting kind." He grinned again. His dimples winked at her, and his hair, black as a raven's wing, was wet and curling around his ears. "But Nate, now, you gotta watch him, he'll bet ya silly and steal ya blind."

"Nate?" She had entered the world beyond hell. Nothing made sense here. Where was The Lone Oak with the Olympic-size swimming pool and the climate-controlled barns?

"My little brother. Won't be home till tomorrow. Come on in before the weather gets bad." He turned away. "You'll want to bring your stuff in right off, 'fore it freezes."

She shook her head once, but he didn't notice. He'd stepped into the adjacent room only to reappear seconds later with a couple of thin towels with which he began rubbing the calf.

"Don't mind telling ya, we're in a little over our heads. Me and Nate, we been working our tail ends off out here. Now I ain't never hired a woman before, but Dad vouched for you, and hell..." He glanced toward her, seeming to size her up as he did so. "You're better looking than old Howard. Dad said you was, but Nate wouldn't believe him, seeing's as how Dad's opinion ain't always reliable. This'll be the first time I beat my little brother in a bet in a good long time. You know, if you'd learn to smile you might be kind of pretty."

She stiffened her back even more. There were those who compared her regal beauty to Cindy Crawford, and then there were those who realized Crawford was far outclassed. "And if you'd change your personality and put a bag over your head you might be halfway appealing yourself. But I doubt it," she said.

Ty stared at her, then settled back on his haunches and laughed.

Rarely had Hannah wanted to strangle anyone as badly as she did now. So before she was hauled off for murder one, she turned on her Armani boots and strode across the porch and down to the Rabbit.

The car door creaked as she opened it. She jolted inside.

It didn't matter where she went. Being murdered by a thug in civilization was surely preferable to *living* here. She twisted the key. The engine coughed once and fell silent.

Hannah closed her eyes, took a deep breath, and tried again. The engine snorted a noise that sounded like a laugh and went still.

"No." She whimpered the word to the windshield and thumped her forehead against the plastic center of the steering wheel, trying once again to pretend this was a nightmare. But she couldn't. It was too cold for her to be asleep.

Eventually there was nothing to do but concede defeat. She stepped back into the storm and slammed the door behind her. It banged closed and bounced open. She slammed it again. It opened again. She grabbed the door, preparing to swing hard enough to vent her frustrations.

"Problems?"

"No!" she snarled, whirling about. Tyrel Fox stood on his porch, looking warm and content. The car door swung lazily open behind her. "No problems. I'm just stuck out here in the middle of nowhere with a grinning Neanderthal and a..." She turned and viciously kicked the door. It closed with a whine and stayed put. "And a rusty heap of junk that won't start!"

"Won't start?" he asked as if surprised. Hooking a thumb into an empty belt loop of his frayed jeans, he leaned against the doorjamb. "Were you planning on leaving?"

Hannah choked out a laugh. "Do I look brain-dead?"

He cocked his head. "Let me think."

Hannah narrowed her eyes at him. "I am leaving." She said the words with careful diction.

"Oh." Ty nodded, glanced at the car, back at her. "Well..." He shrugged. "Too bad things didn't work out," he said, and turning, slammed the door shut behind him.

It was almost twenty minutes before Hannah was convinced she was about to die of hypothermia. The driver's door had refused to open, so she sat in the passenger seat, silently considering what might be said in her eulogy. The problem was, there was not a single soul in this godforsaken state who even knew her real name! And she would *not* be buried as Hannah Nelson!

The wrenching of her pride was a physical ache when she finally exited the car, slogged through the snow, and knocked on the front door.

It opened after what seemed an eternity.

"Hannah!" She hated him for sounding surprised to see her. She'd seen him staring out the window at her at least twice. Once he'd even had the gall to wave and smile.

She gritted her teeth. "My car won't start."

"Really?" He glanced past her toward the Rabbit. "Damn dependable vehicles, too, them Volkswagens. Could be the fuel line. Sometimes they freeze up. Or the spark plugs, maybe, if they got wet. How's your battery acid?"

"I don't..." She paused, smoothing her voice into the dulcet tones they had labored to teach her at Purnell. "I'm sure I couldn't tell you about the state of my battery, Mr. Fox. All I know is that it's supposed to start the car, and it doesn't. I thought you might help me in that regard."

"You want my help?" He motioned toward his chest with a square hand, as if surprised and delighted that she had thought of him.

She nodded once, short and sharp.

His grin was not pretty. "Ask me nicely."

She thought of a thousand things she could do to wipe that

grin off his face and felt somewhat better for each one. "Please," she managed.

He canted his head as if thinking, then said, "You can do better than that."

For just a moment, she was tempted to whap him upside the head. But she wouldn't—not until he'd started her car.

"Please, help me," she said, employing some of the charm she used when Daddy was being difficult.

"That's *better*," he said slowly. "But I can't. I don't know nothing 'bout engines."

"You..." She stopped herself before it got ugly. "What about the fuel—thing—and the battery and—"

"Now Nate," Ty interrupted, lifting a calloused palm toward her, "he's a fine hand with an engine, but he won't be back till tomorrow, like I said."

She was certain he was lying, but there was little she could do about it until she could hire a reliable hit man. She wondered vaguely if Charles Bronson was still in business. "Then might I use your phone to call a garage?" she asked, her tone admirably level.

"Wires must be down somewhere. Phones don't work."

She glared at him, abandoning all civility. "I couldn't possibly stay in this—"

"And even if I was a first-rate mechanic, I don't have no time to fiddle with your car. If I don't get that calf sucking in the next hour or so he's a goner."

Her head was buzzing, but she was coherent enough to know she was lucky he'd cut off her verbal barrage. "Goner?" she asked distractedly.

"Yeah." He looked over his shoulder at the calf. It lay flat out on its side now. "Come from one of my best black heifers, too. That's the second cow I lost already this year."

"How do you lose a cow?" she asked irritably. You'd have to be dumber than a rock to lose something as big as a cow.

"She died," he explained with succinctness.

"Oh." Hannah couldn't help peering past him at the little creature on the floor. Every rib was visible through his ebony coat. "How did she die?" she asked, losing the razor-sharp edge of her anger. Now was not the time to think of lost mothers, she knew. Now was the time to think of a rapid retreat back into sanity. But just then the calf raised its head to stare at her with huge, woeful eyes.

"Is he sick?" Hannah asked, stepping past Ty and into the house.

"Come on in," Ty said belatedly, and closed the door behind her.

"Is he sick?" she asked again.

"Not so's I can tell. But sometimes they just give up when there ain't no mom to love 'em."

"Maybe you should sing to him."

"Sing to him!" She could hear the disbelief in his tone. "I'm afraid I ain't brushed up on my Hank Williams for a while."

She ignored his sarcasm. "Daddy used to sing to me."

"*Daddy?* Hey, where are you from?"

She approached the calf to crouch beside him. His eyes were enormous, his lashes as long as her pinkies, and his coat, when she touched it, was curling as it dried.

"I've never heard a grown woman call her father Daddy. I thought that only happened in the movies. Rich Southern gals who go around saying, 'Oh fiddle dee, Daddy! Why can't I have that Porsche?'"

"If I help you," she said abruptly, glancing over her shoulder at him, "will you help me?"

"Help..."

"With my car."

"Oh. Well, like I said, I'm not much good when it comes to engines...." She opened her mouth, but he lifted a hand to stop her words. "But I tell you what, you get this calf on his feet and eating, and I'll have a look at it."

"Do you have milk for him?"

"Colostrum's what he needs."

She didn't know what colostrum was. Nor did she care. "Well, do you have colostrum, then?" she asked tightly.

"Yeah, Fred just milked out one of his Holsteins. The way my luck's been running, I figured I'd need it sooner or later."

"Then get it," she ordered.

"Dad said you might be the pushy type."

"Pushy?" Hannah rose abruptly to her feet.

Ty was staring at her again, and though she would have preferred to think he looked daft, the truth was quite the opposite. She'd better watch what she said, because Daddy had said Lucky Lindy's henchmen could find her anywhere, even in the frozen tundra of North Dakota if she wasn't careful.

"Dad said you was one of the best riders in the country," Tyrel said, watching her with narrowed eyes.

"Fiddle dee dee. I'm so flattered," she said, using the Southern accent he'd just described.

"In fact, he said you was a pretty good all-around hand."

Hannah pulled her gaze from him and turned toward the calf. "I thought you said he'll die soon if he doesn't eat."

Ty watched her a moment, then nodded. "I'll get a bottle. Meantime, if you really want to get out of here, you might lick the calf dry. That's what the mama would do, ya know," he said, and turned away.

Lick it! Disgust roiled in Hannah's stomach. He couldn't be serious. Or could he? The way he'd cradled the calf against his body, perhaps he was. And she desperately needed to keep the little creature alive so she could buy her ticket out of hell. She grimaced.

But just then Ty's quiet chuckle rolled from the kitchen, and Hannah knew she'd been duped.

She straightened. So he was laughing at her, was he?

No one laughed at her—not since she'd been eight years old. It had been less than a year since her mother's death. She'd just come home from boarding school. She'd gone to the park with her nanny, wearing a pink pinafore and white tights. A boy dressed in jeans and a dirty T-shirt had found something amusing about her attire.

He'd gone home with a bloody nose and a limp.

Tyrel Fox would be lucky if he was walking at all by the time she was through with him.

2

"MILK'S WARM ENOUGH TO... Hey!" Tyrel stopped in the doorway of the kitchen, a large, plastic bottle warm in his hands as he stared at the calf. "He's looking better. How'd you get him up on his chest?"

"I licked him," said Hannah.

Horrified, Ty glanced at the calf, then back at her before realizing she was kidding. One minute in her company had told him she was a spoiled little daddy's girl. But it was also obvious that she was nobody's fool. "It's good to know you can take a joke," he said, approaching her.

"Who wouldn't be amused by your cleverness?" She raised her gaze to his. They were big eyes, slightly almond in shape and as blue as a robin's egg. If the truth be told, she was the kind of woman who took a man's breath away, but there didn't seem to be much reason to tell her that. Her type always knew.

His father hadn't said much about her. She was the daughter of an old friend. Good with horses. Might be temperamental, he'd said. Ty knew now that that was a euphemism for "cowboy killer." He'd tangled with her type when he was in college and didn't feel a need to do so again anytime soon.

She had an attitude, all right. Still, there were advantages to keeping her around, not the least of which was that the old man had said he'd consider it a big favor if Ty would take her on. Since there had been enough bad blood between the two of them, Ty had promised he'd give it a try. And he had, but it hadn't worked out. She'd be gone before morning and

that was definitely for the best. He didn't need a face like
that around to distract...Nate. Neither did he need to listen
to the musical lilt of her voice. It only made him curious
about her. And he didn't want to be curious about his hired
help. He wanted someone like Howard, with a face like an
aged walleye and all the charm to match. Still, as long as she
was there, she could help with the calf.

"I'll prop him on his feet and you try to get him to suck,"
Ty suggested.

Hannah's fingers were slightly spread. He wondered if
she'd been scraping her nails through the calf's hair to sim-
ulate the rough lap of a cow's tongue. Her expression suggested she was neither accustomed to, nor enamored with, the
feel of grime. He stifled a chuckle.

"Dad was a little vague about your experience with cattle," he said, setting the bottle on the floor. "You do know
how to get him to nurse, don't you?"

Hannah rose to her feet. Ty stepped over the calf and, lifting him to the tips of his hooves, encouraged him to stand.

"I'd ask *your* methods," she said, "but I'm afraid I'm not
willing to mimic his mother in this."

Ty remained in stunned silence, then laughed out loud, surprised by her statement and wondering if she had meant to
place such a bawdy suggestion in his mind. When her cheeks
grew flushed, he guessed that she had not. Damn, Howard
hadn't been nearly so appealing when he blushed.

"I think that might be beyond the call of duty," he said.
She reddened more, and he chuckled louder. "Just stick your
finger in his mouth and try to get him to suck."

Grimacing, she glanced at his face as if wondering whether
or not he was pulling her leg again.

"He doesn't have any teeth, ya know. Go ahead."

She did so gingerly, but the calf turned away.

"Try it again," he urged.

"Why would he want to suck on my fingers anyway?" she
asked irritably as she straightened up.

"Reflex. If he don't have a sucking reflex we can kiss him goodbye right off the bat."

He watched her pucker her lips. "There's no reason for him to nurse if he doesn't get something for his efforts. It'd be negative reinforcement."

"Negative—"

"Where do you keep your sugar?" she asked, heading for the kitchen. But when she reached the doorway she stopped in her tracks. Ty winced. Just because he didn't like her didn't mean he wanted her to see his dirty laundry.

"Mr. Fox, are you aware that your kitchen has been ransacked by some maniac?"

Ty turned with the calf still poised between his legs. "We meant to do them dishes before ya got here."

She glanced over her shoulder at him with an arch expression.

"It's not as if we was expecting you to have sole kitchen duties," he said, feeling irritably guilty. His mother would be sorely disappointed if she saw his house. And if she knew he'd exposed a lady to that kind of mess, she'd box his ears. Loretta Fox might look like a fragile house flower, but he'd learned long ago not to get her riled. "Me and Nate's been taught to do our share of housework. We're nineties men. But it's been—"

"Mr. Fox," she interrupted coolly. "Though you insist on believing that I am to be your employee, I assure you there has been a terrible misunderstanding. So it does not concern me what decade, or even what century, you come from."

She then turned and walked into the kitchen. But in truth, Ty couldn't really call it a walk—a slink, perhaps. Though she was dressed in nothing more exotic than snug cotton slacks and a royal blue blouse, she gave the impression that she was draped in silk and gems.

He heard her turn on the tap water and knew she was washing her hands. Then cupboards opened and closed until she reappeared in the doorway with a bowl of sugar.

Picking up the bottle, she knelt in front of the calf. "What are you staring at?" she asked.

"You."

"Well, don't."

"I'm just curious is all. What are planning to do with that sugar, exactly?"

"Daddy used to grind up my pills and add sugar when I was sick."

"Maybe the calf's not as spoiled as you."

Her eyes sparked blue flame when she was angry. Good God, what a face! Nate wouldn't get a lick of work done if she hung around. Luckily she wasn't the type to tough it out. That much he knew.

"I am not spoiled," she said stiffly.

"My mistake."

"I'm sure it's nothing new."

"Go ahead," he urged, nodding to the sugar.

She ignored him as she squirted out a bit of colostrum and smeared it around the nipple. When she rolled it about in the bowl, the sugar stuck to it in a fine layer. Holding the calf's jaw again, she eased the nipple into his mouth.

He chewed at it and turned away. She tried the entire process repeatedly.

Ty watched her. She'd removed her leather jacket and folded back the sleeves of her blouse in two precise rolls. Miraculously, her ivory slacks had not yet taken a single stain. She radiated class and elegance. Who was she? he wondered, but just then the calf began to suck. Wrapping his tongue around the brick-red nipple, he slurped up a bit of the warm liquid.

In another fifteen minutes, she'd convinced him to drink a quarter of the bottle. Hannah raised her eyes to Ty's. They gleamed with bright triumph. A man could be entranced by those eyes, if he didn't know any better. Luckily Ty did.

"Not bad," he admitted. "You learn that trick on your daddy's ranch in Texas?"

The light faded abruptly from her eyes. He watched her stroke the calf's neck before drawing away.

"I'm afraid you have your facts wrong, Mr. Fox. I'm from Colorado."

"Um," he said. "Anyhow, you have my thanks."

She rose to her feet. Ty eased the calf back to the floor.

"And your help," she reminded.

He raised his brows in question.

"With my car."

"Oh, yeah, sure." He hated engines and was about as likely to get that one started as he was to fly to the moon. It almost seemed a better bet to get her to stay the night and head out to wherever she was going first thing in the morning.

"Listen," he said, grateful for her help and sensing her fatigue. "You're never gonna get out of here before dawn. You might as well get a good night's sleep and take off in the morning."

She smiled smugly. "I have to tell you, Mr. Fox, I was expecting a more original line from you."

"Really?" He stiffened, sorry he had ever offered to let her stay. "And that's one of my best ones, too."

"I've heard better."

"Guess them boys in Oklahoma just got me beat all to hell."

"Colorado," she corrected. "And, yes, they do. Now about the car…"

"I told ya I don't know much about engines."

"I doubt that's your sole ineptitude."

Ty snorted as he pulled on his jacket. "Don't let it be said that a Fox don't live up to his end of a bargain."

"Far be it from me to spread such rumors."

"I gotta like the way you talk," Ty said. "Fiddle dee dee. 'Far be it from me to spread such rumors,'" he mimicked. "Did you say that's a New Orleans accent?"

"I said you're a moron," she said sweetly, and slipping into her jacket, hurried out of the house.

Ty followed her, trekking through the accumulating slush

and feeling quite proud that he resisted throttling her. Reaching the car, he pulled up the hood and leaned inside.

"Ahh," he said, looking about.

"What is it?"

"Ohhh."

"Did you find the problem?" she asked, leaning forward to see what he saw.

"Tsk, tsk, tsk," he said, meeting her gaze.

"What is it? What's wrong?"

He shrugged. "I got no idea. But your engine's kind of greasy-looking."

For a moment, he thought she might actually hit him.

"I can't stay here!" she said, sounding panicked.

"Listen, honey," Ty said, leaning against the car's grill. "I understand your predicament. But you don't have to worry. I got myself a gal. Shelly was voted princess for the pork producers of North Dakota just last year, and I'm a one-woman kind of man. I'll keep you at bay no matter how tempted ya get."

Her mouth fell open slightly. She had good straight teeth—and nice long legs. If she were a filly, he'd give her a chance. But as it was, she was just a snooty little girl who thought she was too good for the likes of him. He'd seen her kind before, had mooned over one for more than a year, in fact. And he wasn't in a hurry to do so again.

"Are you suggesting that you think I won't be able to resist you?" she asked.

"Well…" Ty cocked his head and made a crescent shape in the snow with the worn toe of his boot. "Dad said you'd just been jilted and needed to get away for…"

"Jilted!" The word fairly steamed from between her strawberry-tinted lips. "How dare he—the half-witted—"

"Hey, wait a minute. It's what your dad told him."

Her jaw dropped again. But she snapped it quickly closed before pursing her lips and taking a sharp breath through flared nostrils. "Listen here, cowboy," she said slowly. "I have not now, nor have I ever been, jilted."

"Yeah? Then why would your father—"

"He must have misunderstood the circumstances!" she spat. "I needed..." She drew a deep breath. He tried not to grin. "I needed to get away for a while. Daddy was kind enough to call up an old friend. That would be *your* father, I presume, and ask about a job. But I see there has been some terrible mistake. The ranch was supposed to be..." She glanced around the yard at the towering, red milking barn with the slanting lean-tos added on. "Well..." She smiled apologetically, a variation of the expression used for oafs. "You understand."

"No," Ty said, feeling his muscles tense. "I don't."

"Well..." She shrugged. "The ranch was supposed to be...progressive."

"Progressive?" Ty crossed his arms against his chest. He was all for a little sparring—verbal or otherwise. But he really took it personally when someone insulted his ranch.

"I guess you *wouldn't* understand," she said, turning back to him.

Tyrel gritted his teeth. "Try me."

"Where I come from they swim their horses in therapeutic pools." She kicked up a bit of slush that stuck to the leg of his jeans. "Not muck."

"Ahh, Nevada must have really changed since the Dark Ages when I was there."

"Perhaps," she said. "But whatever the case, I have to get back—to Colorado."

"Don't let me stop you."

"But my car—" she cried, then steadied her voice. "My car won't start."

"And my cows need feeding. I guess we all got our problems."

She looked distastefully toward the house, and remained silent for a moment before forcing out her next words. "Where would I sleep?"

"Pardon me?" he said, cocking his head as if he couldn't possibly have heard her correctly.

"I want to know if the accommodations would be satisfactory if I were to stay."

"Lady, you..." Ty chuckled. Glancing at the barn, he shook his head. "You beat all, ya know that?"

"Surely you can't expect me to—"

"Listen! I've changed my mind. You can't stay here after all."

"What?"

"This ain't your type of place. Not anywhere near your standards. You better be on your way."

"But my car! I have nowhere else to go."

Ty smiled slowly. "Then you can sleep in the barn."

"The—"

"The hayloft's pretty cozy really."

"I will *not* sleep in the barn."

They stood in the swirling snow, facing off like snarling badgers. "Then you better be a damn fine cook," Ty said finally. "'Cuz it's the only way I'm going to let you in the house."

"C-cook?" she said.

"Yeah. You cook supper for me I'll let you spend the night."

She shifted her eyes to the house.

"You can cook, can't you?"

"Of course I can cook."

They stared at each other.

Snow was melting on her nose. "All right. It's a deal."

"Good," he said, then turned away. "I'll be in in an hour or so."

"But it's getting dark."

"Funny thing," he said, looking over his shoulder at her. "Them cows still want to eat."

THE KITCHEN WAS A MESS. Worse than a mess. It was disgusting. Dirty dishes were everywhere. There was a half-eaten piece of toast lying jelly-down on the counter. In the refrigerator, Hannah found four aluminum cans, the contents of which she did not care to be privy to. She pushed them aside with a wooden spoon before finally finding a carton of eggs. Drawing them out into the illumination of the single bulb, she gave them a judicial glare.

They looked all right. But then maybe all eggs looked all right. She'd rarely seen an egg that wasn't florentined and garnished. Still, it couldn't be that hard to cook, and she was ravenous.

Breaking six eggs into a prewashed bowl, she managed to get only a bit of shell mixed in with the whites. It was surprising how slippery they were, and more surprising still how they sizzled when they hit the skillet she'd set upon a burner. Covering the pan, she searched for side dishes. She liked croissants with her eggs, but a cursory search proved that such a thing would be far above the contents of Tyrel's kitchen. When she inspected the cupboards, she found a can of french-cut green beans.

A can opener, however, was impossible to locate. Searching the crowded counter, she found a dull knife and a mallet and made do.

Fifteen minutes later, Hannah was feeling quite proud of herself. Proud but filthy. No one with any kind of upbringing at all would eat without bathing first.

Taking the lid from the skillet, Hannah stirred the eggs. They were a bit crispy on the bottom, but surely a barbarian wouldn't expect much. After giving them a thoughtful stir, she glanced through the window toward the barn and considered her options.

It looked as if she really was going to be spending the night in this godforsaken place, so she'd best shower now, before the natives returned.

The bathroom looked only marginally better than the kitchen. Locking the door, she removed her clothes and placed them carefully on the top of the toilet for lack of anywhere better to keep them off the floor. Turning on the shower, she adjusted the temperature and stepped into the bathtub. The water pressure was irritatingly weak, leaving her cold and goose bumped. Finally she closed the drain and slipped down into the accumulating water. It covered her slowly, soothing her with its liquid warmth.

What a day! What a nightmare! She needed a new plan. But what? Sinking her head beneath the surface, she considered every possibility only to discard them one by one. She'd been meticulously careful with her funds. Surely Daddy couldn't have expected her to leave LA without a suitable wardrobe and a full supply of her specially formulated moisturizer. They didn't ship cosmetics from Switzerland for free. And though she didn't regret her purchases, she had very little money left. If she had access to a single one of her credit cards she'd be out of this backwater toilet before Tyrel Fox could conjure up another hard-won thought. But she didn't have a credit card. Not even a checking account. Daddy had insisted that she leave all her identification behind for her own safety.

Sloshing her hair through the water, Hannah felt the silken strands swish against her shoulders and back. She was tired, and the warmth was relaxing, but she had to think or be stuck....

Did she smell something? Hannah went very still, letting her body float to the top of the water as she sniffed. What was that? She thought she'd caught the scent of something. For a moment it had reminded her of Spago's stir-fried vegetable plate. But that was wishful thinking. Could it be...

Smoke!

She scrambled to her feet, splashing water over the side of the tub as she made a wild grab for her clothes. They slipped past her hands. A noise erupted from the kitchen. The toilet cover clattered shut.

In the living room, she heard the calf bellow and furniture fall over.

Dear God, she was burning the house down. Grabbing a towel, Hannah swept it around her body, fumbled with the lock, and rushed toward the kitchen.

In the doorway, she skidded to a halt. Tyrel was there,

stomping the last sparks from a dish towel and running water into her egg pan.

"What the devil!" he roared, then lifted his face to find her standing in stunned silence.

His mouth fell open. A small flame reared up in the dish towel again, but he stomped it out without looking down.

Hannah blinked at him.

"Well," he said, his voice going soft, "if you wanted me so bad you could a just said so, honey. No need to burn down the house to get my attention."

3

"MR. FOX," Hannah said, quieting the rapid beat of her heart as she adopted her well-rehearsed expression of superiority. "I assure you, I'd rather be fricasseed by a short-order cook and served with cheap wine than spend a moment alone with you."

He snorted. "Well, you almost got your wish. 'Cept for the wine part. I'm a Bud man myself. What the hell were you trying to do here?"

She willed herself not to blush and straightened her back. "I was cooking dinner. What have you done to my eggs?"

"Eggs?" He managed to turn away from her long enough to shut off the water flooding over the pan. "Is that what they were?"

"I thought you had chores to do."

"I finished. And a good thing, too. That calf's got champion bloodlines. I'd hate to lose him in a house fire."

She ignored the fact that he neglected mentioning how he'd feel if *she* were burned to cinders. "I was coming to put out the fire," she said, as though his help was neither necessary nor appreciated.

"Yeah," he said, eyeing her. "You could have beat it out with the towel. Course, then you would've been buck naked. You are naked under that towel, aren't you?"

She was silent for a moment. "You, Mr. Fox, have the mind of an adolescent goat."

"And you, Miss Nelson, have really nice..." he began, then let his gaze skim her body, her long, elegant throat, the high rise of her breasts, the endless length of her suntanned legs. "Diction."

She preened a smile at him. "Diction has always been my forte."

"I bet."

"Now if you'll excuse me, I'm going to get dressed."

"So soon?"

She turned with prim elegance. She may be the only woman in the world who could look elegant in a worn, cotton towel. He had planned to replace those old towels with something more substantial. Now he was glad that he hadn't.

In a moment, she was out of sight.

Ty let out a heavy breath and turned back toward the sink. He needed to take some time off. Needed to get away—see that gal of his he'd spouted off about. Only there was no gal. Shelly Madson had given up on him six months ago. All he had now was three hundred head of beef cattle and a couple dozen horses. They were good-looking stock, but they weren't very good company on a cold winter's night. Still, one glance at a woman's bare legs shouldn't be sending him over the edge like this.

He'd better get a grip on himself if he was going to last the night. After all, what was she? Just a woman—and a spoiled woman at that. Her type wasn't for the likes of him, a man who would give up a fine education to return to a broken piece of land in the heart of North Dakota. No, she wasn't his type at—

"Ah-hum."

He heard her clear her throat and turned reluctantly toward the bathroom. She was peeking around the door, the aged towel still wrapped about her torso like damp cheesecloth. Her hair was wet and swung past her shoulder.

It took him a moment to find his voice. "Yeah?" was the best he could come up with.

"I have a small problem," she said stiffly.

In his bathroom there was a half-naked, drop-dead gorgeous woman who was strictly off-limits. He'd been celibate for half an eternity, and *she* had a problem?

"I'd suggest you get dressed before you expound on it," he said.

Her lips pursed and her brows lowered. "Do you think I'd be talking to you in a towel if I could get dressed?"

Now here was an interesting turn of events.

"You can't get dressed?" he asked, feeling his heart rate bump up a tad.

"My clothes..." She paused for a moment, looking irritated and so damned alluring he wanted to weep. Why did the snooty ones always get him all stirred up? "They're wet."

He thought about it for a moment. "Wet?"

"Yes."

"How—"

"That's none of your affair."

He shook his head and approached her, putting a hand on the edge of the door. "Let me in."

"No," she said, holding him out.

Frustration made him push harder until she finally relinquished her hold and he was allowed a glimpse inside.

"Miss Nelson?"

"What?"

"Why did you put your clothes in my toilet?"

Their faces were very close. Hers was pink, but whether from embarrassment or anger was anybody's guess.

"Mr. Fox."

"Yeah?"

"You are a moron." She said the words sweetly.

He grinned. "But I'm not the one who put my pants in the toilet."

"I didn't..." Apparently she'd spoken more loudly than she'd planned, for she lowered her voice and tried again. "I didn't put them in there. They fell."

"Ahhh." He nodded. "And the..." He motioned toward his own chest, for her bra was floating at the top. It was pale pink with a tiny ribbon between the cups. He noticed, though he wished he hadn't. "Did that fall, too?"

"No," she said, and forced a beatific smile. "I threw that in. I figured, as long as the rest was there..." She shrugged.

Nice shoulders.

"Really?" he asked.

She glared at him. "I need some clothes!"

"I bet I'd really tick you off if I asked why, huh?"

"Go!" she growled, then cleared her throat and tried again. "Would you please be so kind as to go out to my car and get my suitcase?"

He frowned and leaned up against the doorjamb. "Maybe if you ask nice. But, hey, I don't know. I mean, you almost burned down my house."

There was a long moment of silence.

"I'm sorry about the fire," she said reluctantly.

He shrugged. "You insulted my ranch."

"Listen!" she steamed, but he held up a hand and canted his head at her. She simmered down quickly, though the fire in her eyes didn't dim a whit. "I'm sorry if I said something to offend your tender sensibilities."

He studied her face. It was golden tan, seamless, cameo perfect. "I like the way you talk. Where did you say you was from?"

She gritted her teeth at him. "Are you going to get my clothes or not?"

"I'm thinking," he said.

But she was, apparently, past watching him think. Swinging the door open, she marched out of the bathroom, past the tottering calf, and toward the front door.

Ty caught up to her just before her hand touched the knob. He slid easily between her and the door. "I was just kidding you."

"Mr. Fox?"

"Yes, Miss Nelson?"

"Have I called you a moron yet?"

"Twice, I think."

"Good. Now if you'll please get out of my way, I'll retrieve my suitcases."

"I'll get them for you."

"I don't want you to get them for me."

"You can't go out there like that."

"Are you sure?"

He grinned. "I'd bet on it."

"How much?"

"Ten bucks."

She smiled primly, like a fragile old lady who had just tasted the perfect tea. "A hundred."

He grinned and swung the door open with a flourish. Snow whistled past him. She blinked and stumbled back.

"Have a go at it, honey," he said.

She took a deep breath, tucked her towel more firmly under itself, and marched out.

Ty watched her go.

Not for a moment did she increase or decrease her pace. Even when her bare feet sunk into the slush, she didn't falter. She had the elegance of a princess and the tenacity of a pit bull. He watched her round the car and wrench the passenger door open. For a moment she bent to retrieve her purse, and though Ty knew he was a cad, he couldn't help wishing she was on the near side of the car when she did so. Still, the view was pretty astounding from where he stood. He'd heard of women skiing in bikinis, but this beat all.

In a moment she was behind the car. The trunk popped open. She dragged out a huge leather suitcase. But just as she did, the towel came loose. Ty held his breath. She dropped her luggage, tucked the towel more securely around her, and wrenched the case from the trunk.

Ty would have helped her get the gargantuan thing up the steps if he could have moved. But the sight of her breasts, crunched between her arms as she struggled with the suitcase, held him immobilized. So she wrestled the thing across the porch and into the house alone.

Though her hair had begun to freeze, the blaze from her

azure eyes looked just about hot enough to melt damn near anything—including his insides.

"Wow!" he said.

"Give me my hundred."

"You don't have any pockets."

The noise she made could only be described as a growl.

Tyrel liked to think he wasn't a total fool, so he turned on his heel and hurried to his bedroom, but by the time he'd dug out four twenties and two tens, she had disappeared into the bathroom with her suitcase.

He couldn't help knocking at the door. Perhaps it was the devil in him. His sister, Joann, had often said he was possessed by a nasty demon. "Mind if I come in?"

"Try it and they won't find your dead body until spring."

"This *is* spring," he countered.

The door burst open. Unfortunately she was an incredibly fast dresser. Perhaps she was a model, he thought. But before he could dwell on that, she had snatched the bills from his hand and was marching barefoot into the kitchen.

She turned in the center of the room. "I'm hungry."

"We've got watered eggs and…" He trailed after her to lift the kettle from the burner. "Charred beans."

She was already rummaging through his cupboards, and in a moment pulled out a bag of potato chips.

"Ahh, veggies," he said, nodding toward the chips as he pulled a six-pack of beer from a shelf. "And protein."

"I don't drink."

"I didn't offer."

They finally sat in silent irritation, her eating stale potato chips and him drinking warm beer.

By the time three cans were empty, Ty felt sick enough to quit, but not drunk enough to ignore her. She was dressed in a chunky yellow sweater and pants that hugged her legs with mouthwatering intimacy.

He was a leg man. Always had been. Now Nate, he went for breasts. And old Pete…

"Where do I sleep?"

Her words stopped his reverie. She'd abandoned the chips and stood beside the table, two-thirds legs and one-half attitude, or something like that. Damn. He was more drunk than he'd thought. He should have put some food into his stomach before swilling beer.

"Where do I sleep?" she repeated.

"How about—"

She stabbed a finger at him. "I wouldn't say it if I were you."

"How do you know what I was going to say?"

"I know your type."

"You sure?"

"Yes. Male."

He laughed. "Up the stairs, first bedroom on the left."

She turned away.

"Miss Nelson," he called.

She turned slowly back.

"Better lock your door in case I get drunk."

A moment later Ty heard the click of her lock.

HANNAH HURRIED through the parking lot. It was dark, and she thought she'd heard a noise behind her. Perhaps she shouldn't have ditched her bodyguard. Daddy had said her life was in danger. But he had always been prone to dramatics. Surely...

The hand seemed to reach out from nowhere. She spun toward her assailant. Images flashed through her mind—a dark beard, straight teeth, a perfect nose. Something familiar about him! But already he had his arm around her body, twisting her away from him, pulling her back up hard against his chest. She shrieked—and awoke with a start.

"You're right. She is better looking than Howard."

Hannah gasped, pulling the coverlet to her chin. "What are you doing in my room?"

"Nice accent, too. Where's she from?"

Ty shrugged. Beside him stood a man in his early twenties.

His hair was brown, but other than that he could have been Ty's twin.

"Dad said Colorado."

"I've never heard an accent like that from Colorado."

"You owe me ten bucks."

"What are you doing in my room?" Hannah asked again.

"The lock don't work. Never has," Ty said, holding out his hand to accept his brother's lost wager.

"Get out!"

"All right. But Nate's going to be heading out soon. Either he looks at your car right off or it's gonna be too late."

"Get out!"

"Okay."

Both men exited the room. It took Hannah less than two seconds to react. This was her chance to leave!

She was dressed and out the door in a minute. The uncarpeted stairs were cold against her bare feet. She stopped at the sight of the snow outside, then slipped into an oversize pair of rubber boots and a parka that waited by the door.

Both men stood with their heads together under the hood of her Rabbit.

Wrapping the parka more closely about her body, she hurried over to them. The wind had died down, but it was still bitterly cold. Waiting, she shifted from foot to foot.

Eventually Nate looked up.

"Well?" she said.

"We can do the kind thing, and put it out of its misery right here and now. Or we can send it to town and see if they can save it. But I'm afraid that would only make it a long and painful death."

She scowled at him. It was cold, she was tired, and she was in North Dakota with a pair of cowboys who thought they were funny. None of these things made her happy.

"How much would it cost?" she inquired.

"To resurrect it?" Nate asked.

She gritted her teeth, held on to her patience, and nodded.

"I don't know. Maybe eight, nine hundred dollars."

"Eight or nine—" she squawked.

"I could be wrong," Nate said.

"How wrong?"

"Could be closer to fifteen hundred."

"Dollars? I don't have fifteen hundred dollars."

Nate shrugged. "Sorry."

She swept the hair out of her eyes. "What am I supposed to do now?"

"'Scuse me but..." Nate shoved his hands deep into the pockets of his jeans. "Weren't you gonna work on the farm here—"

"Nope." Ty cut him off. "Where Miss Nelson comes from they swim their horses in pools, not in muck. Isn't that right, honey?"

Hannah didn't even bother to glare at him. "What could I get for it?"

"The car?" Nate looked doubtful, if not pained. "I'm afraid you might have to pay them to haul it away."

Ty chuckled.

Now she glared at him. "What would it take to buy a plane ticket?"

"From where?" Nate asked, looking befuddled.

"To where?" Ty chortled.

"To anywhere but here!"

"How much do you have?" Nate asked.

"That's none of your business."

"That means she's busted," Ty said.

"I've got *your* hundred," she corrected.

"What's that?" Nate asked.

"Never mind," Ty said.

"I could give you a ride into the Valley," Nate offered.

"How could I get out of there?"

Nate shrugged again. "Hitchhike?"

"Hitchhike!" Hannah gasped. None of this could be real. No more real than the nightmare that tormented her. But the nightmare *was* real.

"Listen, Hannah," Ty said, sounding serious now. "There

are a couple decent restaurants in town. You could waitress there till you get enough cash.''

"Waitress!"

"Well, why couldn't she just work here?" Nate asked.

"No!" Ty said, emphatically shaking his head.

"Why not?" Nate inquired.

"She's…" Ty shrugged. "She's too good for us."

Hannah studied him for a moment. "You think I can't do it.''

"No. That's not it," Ty said.

"It is. You think I can't do the work!" she persisted.

"Well, yeah! Yeah, I do!" Ty agreed. "You in your prissy little boots and your—"

"A thousand a month plus room and board," she interrupted. "That's what was agreed upon. Am I correct?"

"Well, yeah," Nate said.

"No!" Ty argued. "That was only if it worked out, and this ain't working out!"

"Oh, come on, Ty. She's down on her luck!"

"She is not down on her luck. She's *bad* luck!" Ty argued. "You can take my word for it. I know her type."

"The calf wouldn't suck for *me* this morning, either."

Ty scowled. "I suppose you think he's mourning Miss Fancy Pants, here."

Nate shrugged, grinning slightly. "Could be."

"No, it—"

"I can get him to eat," Hannah interrupted.

"The hell you can!" Ty countered.

"He'll eat."

Ty snorted.

"If I can't keep him alive and healthy for the next two weeks you don't have to pay me. But if I do, you owe me twice the agreed salary and a ride to the nearest town."

"That sounds fair," Nate ventured.

"It doesn't sound fair," Ty argued. "It sounds crazy. You think she can just sit around and look…irritating, and it will be fine just so long as she keeps one little calf alive and I'll give her a thousand bucks.''

"I can do the work," she said. "Whatever needs to be done."

He stared at her in silence for a moment, then said, "Hell, this here's a four-man ranch, short about two men."

"Could be she's worth two men," Nate said, grinning. "Come on. You promised Dad."

Ty ground his teeth, then threw up his hands. "All right. Fine. You win," he said, turning away. "But if she burns down the house, we lynch her."

Hannah watched him march off toward the barn.

"He was just leggin' ya," Nate said. "I think he likes you."

"Believe me, Mr. Fox," she said, turning stiffly toward him. "I couldn't care less if he likes me or not."

"Well, good. 'Cuz he's gonna act like he don't," Nate said, and followed his brother into the cattle yards.

Hannah blew out a heavy breath. She'd won. She would work at The Lone Oak just as...

Wait a minute. What had she done? She didn't want to stay here. She wanted to leave. They'd tricked her into staying, but it wasn't going to work. She was going to leave. Now!

Storming back into the house, Hannah slammed the door behind her.

The calf lurched unsteadily to his feet and blinked at her with huge, blue-black eyes. Hannah stumbled to a halt. If a calf could cry, she would swear this one was about to.

Lowering its round little head, it let out a tiny bellow. It was a pathetic sound. Hannah bit her lip.

The calf stumbled toward her, its tattered umbilical cord swaying as it came.

"Are you hungry?"

The calf bellowed again, the sound so weak and low it was barely audible, but the effort was enough to make him wobble on his feet. The imbalance made its uneven hooves slip on the yellowed linoleum, and in a moment it fell in a heap on the floor.

Hannah rushed to him. It lay hopelessly on its side and stared at her with limpid eyes.

"Poor baby," she crooned, squatting down to scratch his neck. Her own tears felt ridiculously close to the surface. But it was just because she was angry, of course. Angry and frustrated. "Are you okay? You must be lonely, losing your mother. In here alone with—"

A noise distracted her. Hannah brought her head up with a snap. Tyrel Fox stood in the doorway, watching her.

She got to her feet. Silence stretched between them. She cleared her throat and looked over the calf.

"I think he's lonely."

Despite her expectations, he didn't laugh at her. "Could be. But he's for sure hungry."

Tyrel's eyes were coffee brown and his expression somber as he watched her.

The scrutiny was making her nervous. "I thought you were busy outside."

"Thought I'd better show you where to find the colostrum and stuff."

"Oh." Despite her best efforts, she could come up with nothing more scathing.

Their gazes locked.

He pulled his away. "It's, uh…" He scratched the back of his neck where his hair brushed his collar and strode toward the kitchen. "It's in here."

She trailed after him, noticing as she entered that inhospitable domain that its condition had not improved since her last sojourn there.

"We keep it frozen," he said, opening the freezer. Four plastic pint containers stood between an empty ice tray and an open bag of corn that had spilled frosted kernels onto the deck. He cleared his throat. "We meant to get that cleaned up."

She said nothing.

"Anyway..." Taking out one pint container, he closed the freezer and reached into the open drawer below the oven with his other hand. Not surprisingly, it was empty but for five dried noodles and a small charred puddle of something unidentifiable. "We meant to get them pans cleaned, too."

He was looking at her strangely, she thought, as though he could read her thoughts, see into her soul. It made her uncomfortable at best, panicked at worst. She straightened her back.

"Listen, Mr. Fox, despite all your failed intentions, I'm certain I can manage to feed Daniel if you'll simply explain the procedure."

The ice queen was back. Tyrel snapped his attention onto that one fact. For a moment he could not fail but see the vulnerability in her eyes, but now she had it locked away. And a good thing, too, he told himself as he knocked last night's charred beans into the trash, rinsed the pan, and filled it halfway with water.

"Daniel?" he asked, suddenly realizing she had used that name.

She almost backed up a step, as though he had surprised her. She pursed her lips, looking defensive, and in that one wild moment, he wondered what it would be like to kiss her.

God, he had to get out more.

"Daniel?" he said again, and managed, just barely, to sound mocking instead of smitten.

"His eyes. They remind me of Daniel Day-Lewis."

He would never understand how she could manage to make it sound as if he were daft not to have realized the resemblance himself.

"Have you seen *The Last of the Mohicans?*"

He shook his head and steadied his brain. She was wearing a pair of blue jeans that did things most jeans didn't do. "I think I missed that movie."

"Then you wouldn't understand," she said, and paced to the stove. "What do I do with the water?"

"You boil it." He stared at her. Her face was very close

now. She had scrubbed off her makeup, or maybe she had never worn any, but still, even in the harsh morning light that streamed through the east window, her complexion looked perfect and her eyes huge and gleaming. It made him all the more irritable, especially since his own face was unshaven and his eyes felt as though they had been sandblasted and spray painted. "You can boil water, can't you?"

She smiled at him. Perfect teeth. His felt slimy. "Of course I can boil water," she said.

"Well, I didn't know," he said, turning on the burner, "after last night."

"I assure you, last night was merely an unfortunate accident."

"Then you can cook?" He watched her face.

"Of course I can." She didn't meet his eyes.

He couldn't help but chuckle. Somehow it made him feel better to know she was lying, to know she had faults...besides her personality. "Yeah, well," he said, "maybe we'll let Nate cook. He's pretty good—"

"I can cook!" she said, glaring at him.

"Then you won't mind making dinner?" he asked. He couldn't help himself. Everything about her got him riled up.

"Dinner?" She raised her brows at him. "Isn't it a bit early to be considering dinner?"

"You might call it lunch," he said, and thumping the frozen pint into the pan, turned to go. "But whatever it is, we usually have it about noon."

"You're expecting me to cook for you?"

He turned. "You said you could. Said you could do any work that needs doing. So I guess the kitchen will need some cleaning. You'll find meat and vegetables frozen in the deep freeze in the basement. I'm a meat-and-potatoes kind of man. Oh, and watch that colostrum. You don't want to burn the house down," he said, and smiling, left her to her own devices.

Three hours later, Hannah disagreed completely; burning down the house was not a bad idea at all. It had taken her over an hour to get the calf to drink, and then he'd only consumed a little. She'd worried that he was weakening and had gone into the living room to check on him. He'd lain flat on his side again, so she'd covered him with the parka she'd worn outside this morning. She hoped it was Ty's and that Daniel did disgusting things to it.

But even with her worries about the calf, Daniel was still the bright spot of her day. The kitchen, on the other hand... She swayed in the doorway, on her way back from returning a boot to the hall. Why it had been in the sink, she couldn't say. But it was past eleven o'clock, the place was still a mess, and she hadn't started lunch.

Taking a fortifying breath, she made her way across the kitchen to the basement door. Once in the bowels of the old house, she searched for a light, found one bare bulb operated by pulling a string, and proceeded to rummage around in the huge, chest freezer. After several minutes and minor frostbite, she pulled out two rock-hard packages wrapped in white paper and marked *steak*.

Frozen peas were easier to find and identify.

Stumbling over indistinguishable piles of everything on her way to the stairs, she caught sight of a bag of potatoes. Dragging it along with her, she stumbled back into the light of day and set to work.

Half an hour later, Hannah was quite proud of herself. The steaks were in the oven, the potatoes mashed and the peas cooking.

In the living room, Daniel had rolled onto his chest and was peering rather cheekily into the kitchen, so she heated more milk, poured it into a clean bottle and went over to him.

It took several minutes to get him to show the least bit of interest. But after his initial taste, he staggered to his feet and drank a bit before flopping back to the floor.

The door creaked open. Hannah glanced up.

"See," Nate said, stepping inside in front of his brother. "I told ya he'd come around for her."

Ty grunted and hung his hat on a nearby peg, then finding

no more available spots, dropped his jacket by the door. "How much did he drink?"

She shrugged, feeling strangely self-conscious. "A half a cup maybe."

"He's never going to make it like that."

"He will, too." She was on her feet in a moment, and though she called herself a thousand kinds of fool, she felt tears sting her eyes.

The two men stared at her as if she'd grown an extra head.

"He will, too," she said, more softly now. "He's not going to die."

Nate cleared his throat. Ty glanced toward the kitchen.

"Dinner ready?"

Despite herself, Hannah was grateful for the change of subject. Nodding, she covered the calf again, and hurried through the doorway to the oven.

The men followed. Seeing she'd neglected to set the table, but delighted to find a trio of clean, mismatched plates near the sink, they distributed the crockery, then stood beside their chairs, looking anything but at ease.

She glanced toward them, then turned swiftly away, wondering with some anxiety, what she should do next.

She cleared her throat. "Sit down," she said.

They did so, bumbling with their chairs before settling in. In a moment she had the steaks out of the oven and deposited on their plates. As for herself, she was too nervous to eat, so she rushed back to the stove for the potatoes.

The men were bent over their plates, so she deposited the pan on the table and hurried away in search of a serving spoon.

"Hey!" said Ty suddenly. She turned to half standing as he lifted the pot in his right hand. The vinyl tablecloth came with it, but finally gave way, leaving a perfectly melted, pan-shaped hole where the table now showed through.

"Oh!" Hannah murmured.

Ty stared at her, then settled back into his chair. "It's, uh, an old tablecloth," he grumbled.

Nate was staring at his brother with raised brows. Ty glared at him. Nate grinned, then said, "Yeah, and happily sacrificed for a good meal. Mashed potatoes," he crooned. Taking the pan from Tyrel, he peeked inside. His brows raised even farther. "Or not."

Hannah rubbed her hands nervously against her thighs. "They, umm… They were quite hard. It made them difficult to mash."

Both men were staring at her again.

"Some people cook them before they mash 'em," Nate said.

"Oh."

"It's not necessary, ya understand," he added.

"God help us," Ty said.

Hannah propped her fists on her hips. "What's that supposed to mean?"

"Nothing," Ty said, raising his hands in surrender.

Frustration boiled with a thousand other emotions in Hannah. "Eat your steak," she said.

"Sure," Ty responded, setting his knife to the meat. "I like mine frozen in the middle."

4

"WHAT THE HELL!" Ty shouted, racing into the house.

Sparks were shooting from the microwave like a light show gone mad. Shielding his eyes with one hand, he gathered his nerve and punched a button.

The blue sparks faded to oblivion, but his temper did not. It had only been a few hours since he'd forced himself to eat half-frozen steaks. Now this!

"What the hell are you doing?" he shouted into the living room.

Hannah sat on the floor beside an empty milk bottle. It was obvious she'd fallen asleep there. A crease bisected the smooth skin of her cheek where it had rested on the parka, her hair was messed, and one slim hand still rested on the calf's back, but it was her eyes that held his attention. They were as large and soft as a fawn's.

"What?" she asked, looking disoriented...and vulnerable.

Vulnerability. It seemed a strange attribute for this woman who could slash him to shreds with nothing more than a word or a glance. And yet it was there in her expression, just as he had seen her earlier when she'd been talking to the calf.

He tried to remember his anger, but it had burned to ash now, with only a bit of heat left to punctuate his words. "What were you doing?"

She rose to her feet. The calf rose with her.

"I was defrosting the casserole...as instructed." It took her a moment, but she could draw dignity around her like a magical cloak. Even half asleep, obviously in the wrong, and caught dead to rights, she could look like an offended queen.

"Mom puts tin foil between the layers," he said. "You have to take it out before you defrost it. Didn't they teach you anything in…" He eyed her. Seeing her like that, with her defenses only half in place and her eyes sleep-softened, took his breath away. Maybe she *was* royalty. "London?" he guessed.

She strode toward him. "Colorado," she corrected. He watched her enter the kitchen and noticed for the first time that she had cleaned it. Well, actually what she had done was wash some of the dishes and stuff everything else into a broken laundry basket. "And I did *not* put tin foil in the—"

Her mouth fell open. Her fair brows rose.

The microwave oven stood open, its door melted, its walls singed.

"Oh."

"Yeah." He stared at her, trying to resurrect his anger. His *justifiable* anger. "Oh."

"You should have told me the appliance was defective," she said, turning toward him.

"It wasn't defective."

She propped her hands on her hips, looking accusatory. "There's a hole in the door. Obviously it's defective."

He prepared to voice an objection, but instead drew a deep breath, took off his hat and ran his fingers through his hair. "You're right, of course. I should have noticed that," he said. "Listen, Hannah, I don't have time to argue. I've got a hell of a mess out there. Houdini got in with the heifers again. One cow's calving, three more look like they're going to come in tonight, and there's a storm blowing out of the northwest."

"Houdini?"

"HV Black Sultan's his registered name. A bull," he explained. "Best, winningest and most irritating animal I've ever paid good money for. We've got to get him out of the heifer pen."

She blinked, and somehow, against all odds, he couldn't help but think of long afternoons spent in her arms. Her skin would feel like sun-warmed satin beneath his fingers, and her laughter would trickle through his system like primitive music. They would kiss and...

"Heifer pen?" she said, blinking sleepily.

"Yeah." He was beginning to sweat, and wondered vaguely if it was because of his outdoor clothes or her proximity. When he was done calving he was going to find himself a girlfriend, get laid, spend a month in bed and *not* think about Hannah Nelson's Audrey Hepburn eyes ever again. "Yeah, them heifers don't know much 'bout safe sex and if we don't get Houdini out of there we're going to have babies having babies in December. Or he might get himself banged up and then his chances at the stock show would be shot all to hell."

"That'd be bad?"

"It wouldn't make my life any easier."

"I'd offer to help," she said. "But I'm afraid you've ruined dinner again and I'll have to find something else to—"

"Get your coat," he interrupted, glad he could save himself from one more of her failed attempts at cooking. "Your training begins now."

HOUDINI LOOKED rather like an overstuffed plush animal. He was very large, very black and very determined to stay with his young harem. But with shouts and a few whacks on the head from the wooden canes they'd armed themselves with, he was convinced to abandon the heifers and lumber back into his own quarters, a bachelor pad he shared with eight other bulls.

Hannah stood in the muck that rose nearly above her borrowed rubber boots and squinted against the swirling snow. "Now what?" she yelled over the wind.

"Come on," Tyrel shouted back.

They trekked together through the darkness with the snow whirling around them. Finally they reached a long, deep building. It was no more than three walls and a roof, really, but it kept the wind at bay, making it seem unreasonably cozy. There was a row of lights on the ceiling, and by their glow, Hannah saw the cattle. They were lying on their sides with their legs curled beneath them, grunting softly as they chewed their cuds. Calves lay beside them, looking content and sleepy, like tiny kittens curled into the straw.

"Pretty," she said softly.

"What?"

She scanned the herd, then carefully shut away any tender feelings this scene might evoke and raised her voice. "Pretty...many cattle," she said.

"Yeah. Two, three hundred all together. But it'll be a whole lot less if we don't get 'em bedded down good. Pneumonia can put a hell of a dent in a cow herd."

He led the way through the barn, weaving around the clusters of cows that felt no need to move more than their heads to allow them past. Toward the back of the building there were huge, rolled bales of sunshine yellow. Hannah stared at them.

"Here's the deal," Ty said. "We cut the twine strings, unroll the straw, and spread it out nice and soft."

For the next hour that's what they did, working their way around the bovine. Finally they were finished. Hannah leaned against the wall, pitchfork in hand, to watch a pair of calves, their tails kinked high in the air as they frolicked in the fresh bedding.

"Pretty," he said quietly.

"What?" She glanced at Ty. He didn't look away, but stared into her eyes. Self-consciously, she pressed a few strands of half-frozen hair back under her borrowed hood. After this little stint, she was going to spend a whole week at the spa, have everything that could be conditioned conditioned, and never think of Tyrel's whiskey-rough voice again. "What?" she repeated.

"It's pretty late," he said. "We better get going."

"Where?" Her back ached and her stomach was grumbling. When was the last time she'd had a decent meal? Spago's beckoned.

"Know anything about horses?" Ty asked.

Even bundled up like an underweight abominable snowman in borrowed clothes, she could look like a misplaced queen, Ty noticed, and wasn't at all happy about the knowledge.

"I believe that's what you hired me for," she said.

There was silence for a moment, except for the keening wind.

"Yeah," Ty said. "Come on."

The trek through the cow pens was not a pleasant one, but in a few minutes they stepped into the horse barn. He fought the door closed behind them. It took a moment to adjust to being out of the wind, and by then he'd flipped on the lights.

Horses blinked at them from the stalls that lined a clean swept concrete aisle. Country music crooned from an unseen source.

"If I give you a list of their rations, can you feed them?" Tyrel asked.

She gazed at the rows of faces behind the stall bars then back at him. "Why do you insist on thinking I'm daft?"

"I don't know," he said. "Maybe it has something to do with the microwave or the kitchen fire or—"

"I can feed them," she interrupted, looking irritable.

He grinned, then turned and went into a room to the left of where they were standing.

"Grain's in here," he said, opening the feed bin.

She surveyed the tack room, but didn't comment on its immaculate appearance. Apparently the good fairy that cleaned the barn had been frightened off by the sight of the house. Moving on, she peered into the wooden box that contained the horse feed. "Rather rich for pregnant mares, isn't it?" she asked, scooping a handful into one palm.

"You know horses?" he asked in surprise.

"That's what you hired me for," she repeated.

"Oh, yeah, that's right. And here I keep thinking it's 'cuz of your sweet personality."

She smiled grittily. "Fiddle dee dee."

"Or because of the way you look in a pair of jeans."

"Well, shucks, Mr. Fox, you'd look good, too, if—"

"I didn't say you look good," he said. "I just meant someone as skinny as you isn't likely to distract Nate."

He watched fire spark in her eyes. "I'm so sorry I can't live up to your pork queen's measurements."

"That's pork princess," he corrected.

"My mistake. But I have to tell you, Mr. Fox, you're no Mel Gibson."

He snorted. "It gets pretty lonely here in the northland, honey. By summer I'll look like Tom Cruise to you."

"You already do," she said. "Did you see *Interview with the Vampire?*"

He scowled. "No, I missed that one, too."

"Too bad."

"Umm," he said. "Should I assume he was the vampire?"

"With fangs and everything."

"Really?" They were very close. "And I hardly ever bite anyone."

"I'll remember to thank my lucky stars."

"Or…" he said, leaning a fraction of an inch closer. "Was he one of them seductive kind of monsters?"

For a moment, she said nothing, but then she looked away. "So how much do I feed them, anyway?"

He should laugh at her sudden nervousness, he thought. But as it was, he was standing so close to her he could barely breathe. Somehow it seemed that all the air had been sucked out of his lungs. He cleared his throat. "Here's the list of rations," he said, pointing to the typed and laminated paper tacked to the wall. His arm brushed hers. A spurt of excitement rushed up his spine. He jerked his arm away.

What the hell was wrong with him? He was acting like a twelve-year-old kid with his first crush. And she wasn't the kindly librarian type to let him down easy. If he gave her so much as a clue to his feelings, she was likely to smack him up against the wall and spit in his eye. The thought made him irritable. "You think you can do this without screwing up?" he asked.

Hannah drew back a pace. She felt like the Michelin Man on steroids. It was hard to manage a good haughty expression in this ridiculous getup, but she did her best.

"I have two options here," she said. "I can hire a hit man, or I can pretend you didn't say that."

He snorted. "Listen. I don't mind you poisoning me and my brother, but don't mess up with the horses. Got it?"

"Fiddle dee dee. Charmed yet again," she said. "Do you have rolled oats for the mares?"

He stared at her. "Like I said, the list of rations is there."

"The mares are going to get impacted if you don't give them more fiber."

"They never have yet."

"Colonel Shelby says—"

"Colonel Shelby?" he asked, using her own tone on her.

"Never mind." She turned away. "You're the expert, of course."

"*Colonel* Shelby? Who could that be, I wonder? Your father, your lover, your dog?" he asked, following her to the row of bridles that hung on the wall.

"No one to concern yourself with."

"Your parrot, your piano teacher, your... Your riding instructor!" he said, sounding as if he was certain of himself.

She stiffened. Daddy had warned her to be careful. "No. You were right. He's my parrot."

"He's your riding instructor," he argued. "In New York."

She breathed a snort through her nose, hoping she sounded derisive.

"In Maryland, Kentucky, LA?"

"That's right," she said, turning to him. "He was my riding instructor in Los Angeles." She put one mittened hand dramatically to her heart. "Oh, the rides we used to share. Just the colonel and I in Central Park."

"Central Park's in New York."

"Could it have been Hyde Park?"

"London."

"Glacier Park?"

"Montana."

"Oh. Maybe it wasn't Colonel Shelby at all. I think it was Mary Poppins."

"Fine," Ty said. "Don't tell me. Just take care of the horses. Feed 'em and clean their stalls."

"Clean their stalls!"

He smiled. She would have liked to have said it was an ugly smile. Instead, it curled the edges of his mouth up enough just to call it entrancing. "Yeah. The wheelbarrow's right there. And the manure... Well, just follow your nose."

"Wait a minute, I didn't—"

"Yeah, you did. Anything that needs doing I believe was the agreement. The stallion's got his own corral beside the heifer pen. Feed him inside. And don't forget the herd out back."

"Out back?" she asked. "You mean you have horses outside in this weather?"

"That's right." Tyrel opened the door. "Barn's not big enough for all of them. This ain't no ride in the park—Central or Hyde." He looked over his shoulder at her. "Welcome to North Dakota," he said, and stepped outside.

HANNAH STAGGERED through the snow toward the house. Her toes were frozen, every muscle ached, and if Spago's had even given her linguine that looked as limp as her arms felt, she'd send it straight back.

Perhaps she should help Tyrel with the rest of his chores, but if she spent one more minute in the cold she was going to freeze up and turn blue like a therapeutic eye mask. Still, when she opened the door, guilt made her stop and squint at the barn.

"Close the door. You're letting the snow in."

She turned slowly.

From the kitchen Ty grinned at her. He looked warm and toasty in his stocking feet. His square hands were wrapped around a steaming mug and his blue-black hair was brushed back behind his ears. He had funny ears, small, flat on the top, and for one crazed moment she could think of nothing but boxing them.

"How long have you been in here?" Her voice sounded rather gritty, she noticed.

"Oh, I don't know. Two, three hours maybe, huh, Nate?" He turned toward the kitchen.

His brother, just visible as he passed the door, blew on his coffee and snorted. His nose was still red from the cold.

"Damn!" Ty said. "You look chilled to the bone. Nate warmed up some soup. Want some?"

She blinked at him. Her eyelashes, she noticed suddenly, were frozen in clumps. "I hate you."

He laughed. "But I'll grow on you if you stay around long enough."

"In that case I'll be leaving in the morning."

"But your car don't start."

"I'll walk."

He laughed again. "It don't look like you're gonna be walking far tomorrow. In fact, the way you look, I'll be surprised if you get out of bed at all. Want some soup?"

She didn't answer, but silently peeled off her sleet-covered coat and thought of various ways to dismember him.

"No?" he said. "It's pretty good. How 'bout some coffee?"

Removing the hooded, zip-up sweatshirt, she let it drop to the floor. It had a hole in the pocket and smelled distinctly of cow manure. Looking down, she saw that her socks had somehow gotten wet and were now stained a strange sort of parchment yellow. It seemed a sad commentary on the decline of her life.

"I'm going to take a bath." She said the words more to herself than to him.

"Really? Need any help?" he asked, watching her cross the living room toward the stairs.

"Mr. Fox," she said, turning to stare at him point-blank.

"Yes, Ms. Nelson?"

"I have something to tell you."

"I wait with bated breath."

"I have Mace in my purse. The first…" She glared at him, then glared at Nate who appeared in the doorway behind him. "The first *creature* who comes through that bathroom door is going to get a blast up his nose."

"Oh." Ty gave her an expression of mock fear that he almost managed to let overtake his grin. "But what if you fall asleep?"

"Then maybe I'll be lucky and drown before I wake up here again," she said, then marched up the stairs.

TRUE, THE WATER PRESSURE was still pathetic, but the warmth was heavenly. It seeped into Hannah's very soul, easing her muscles, melting her aches.

Her hair floated around her shoulders and arms. She released a heavy sigh. She couldn't go on like this. She was simply going to swallow her pride and beg Daddy for help. True, a Clifton Vandegard should never have to apologize to anyone. But she would even do that if Daddy would send her enough money to get home.

But where was Daddy? He'd said that he, too, had to disappear. That LA wasn't safe for either of them anymore. Her throat contracted. She'd never meant to cause trouble for him, and if he were hurt…

She refused to allow herself to think any further along those lines. George Vandegard was still a powerful man. He could take care of himself. Always had. He had never needed her—except as his little showpiece—the product of the perfect union between European class and American drive. His little princess, rewarded when she was pretty, when she curtsied, when she smiled just so for the cameras. Or so it had seemed to a lonely, out-of-place child with no friends and no understanding that she should even long for some.

Now she wondered. For in the past couple of years, her father had aged, mellowed maybe. Sometimes she would find him watching her with a strange melancholy expression that, if she had been raised differently, might have enabled her to ask him to share his thoughts, and to share her own with him.

But she hadn't. She had grown up emotionally independent and environmentally disabled. She could accessorize like a supermodel, she could exchange dry witticisms with dukes and megastars, but she couldn't microwave a meat loaf.

In short, she was unequipped for life.

It seemed strange now that she hadn't realized that before. While she'd been learning what kind of hat looked pert yet sophisticated, her peers had been learning how to live.

She was good at nothing.

Weariness sloshed over her, but even so, she knew her thoughts were not quite the truth. She was good at something. She was a fine equestrienne. Colonel Shelby had said so enough times. She had good hands, a firm seat and balance extraordinary, he had said with the fervor of a zealot. But— if she was going to reach Olympic standards, she would have to learn to be selfless, to sacrifice. She would have to have heart.

And so she had quit, because if she wanted heart, Daddy could sure enough go buy her one. She didn't need the aggravation. And she had done just fine without Colonel Shelby and his nagging. Skiing trips, shopping and facials could more than fill her days. She had been perfectly content until that night in the parking lot.

But she was safe now.

Her mind felt fuzzy. Daddy had hired a new chef. Perhaps she'd have crepes for breakfast. Sleep settled in like a cloud of cotton, cushioning her body, soothing her nerves.

Time passed softly until the sound of a door opening nibbled at her consciousness. A noise followed that sounded strangely like tiny hooves on linoleum.

"You wouldn't Mace a movie star, would you?"

Hannah awoke with a start, and grabbed for the shower curtain. There was a scraping sound, and suddenly the whole thing, rod and all, splattered into the tub.

She shrieked, shocked as cool water splashed onto her face.

"Hannah!" Ty said, thumping the door wide and torpedoing into the bathroom. "Are you…" he began, but suddenly his words came to an end. His lips turned up into a satyrlike smile, and he laughed.

Reality hit Hannah like ice water. She wasn't with Daddy. She wouldn't have crepes for breakfast, and she was still in hell. Glaring past the edge of the downed shower curtain that draped her body, Hannah raised an arm at him.

"Out!"

He only laughed harder, bending over now to guffaw his glee.

"Out!" she shrieked.

He reached for the vanity, his hand shaky from his laughter, and drew a towel to his eyes. "If Howard had been half so entertaining, I'd a begged him to stay."

She wasn't going to hire a hit man. She was going to do the job herself. And she was going to enjoy it.

"I'm…I'm sorry," he said, apparently trying to control his jocularity. "But I just…" Laughter again. "Your movie star…"

She would kill him slowly—smother him with the shower curtain, rather like the guy that had fallen into the swimming pool in the first *Lethal Weapon.*

Tyrel motioned behind him, and Hannah saw now that the little, knock-kneed calf stood in the doorway, looking bewildered. "Daniel Day-Lewis is hungry. I brought you up a bottle," Ty said, righting the nippled thing that dripped milk onto the narrow vanity. Apparently he'd tossed it there when she'd screamed.

She allowed sanity to creep in. She couldn't kill him now. She'd have to get dressed first.

"I'll feed him downstairs," she said, gathering the shreds of her dignity.

He stood in silence for a moment, watching her with a crooked grin. She slicked her hair back and defiantly held his gaze. She must look a sight, no makeup, dressed in a crusty shower curtain and deflating soap bubbles.

"I can feed him for you," he said. "You look tired."

She straightened. "I'm sorry my appearance isn't up to your lofty standards," she said. "I'll feed the calf."

"I don't mind," he countered.

For a moment silence lay gently between them, but then she remembered herself. "It's not going to be that easy to back out of our agreement," she said. "That calf is going to live, and he's going to live because of me." She jabbed a thumb toward her chest. Water splashed into her eye. She ignored it for the sake of dignity—a slippery thing lately. "You'll be paying me a thousand dollars and I'll be leaving this backwater toilet on the first plane."

He snorted and bending, lifted Daniel easily into his arms. "Okay. If that's the way you want it." He turned, then stopped in the doorway. "Oh, breakfast is at six. I like my eggs over easy."

OVER EASY! Nothing was easy. Not on this piece of godforsaken tundra.

Hannah groaned as she slid her feet over the edge of the bed and onto the floor. The *cold* floor. The cold, uncarpeted floor.

She didn't have an alarm clock. She'd always regarded them as barbaric, and had insisted on having Maria awaken her with fresh-squeezed orange juice on those rare occasions when she'd had to rise before noon.

But now, despite everything, she had awakened on her own every couple of hours during the night. She didn't know why. Perhaps she was worried about Daniel, whom she'd fed twice since her bath. Or perhaps it was simply because, no matter what, no matter if the sky fell and the sea turned to chocolate mousse, she was not going to let that half-brained, black-haired Neanderthal man beat her.

He liked his eggs over easy! She would cook them to golden perfection, then dump them over easy on his head!

The image of Tyrel Fox with an egg flopped over one odd flat ear, propelled her out of her nightgown and into jeans and a short pink, button-down cardigan. She'd bought it on a Christmas trip to London. Derik had said it made her look like a million dollars.

Derik was an Englishman, with an Englishman's dry wit and fashionably narrow build. She'd thought herself in love with him. Her first love really, and had decided with a virgin's determination to make him her first lover.

Their kisses had been hot and impassioned. Or so she thought. Too hot. Hot enough to scare her. She had apologetically called a halt. The following morning he'd told his cronies that she'd had to quit before her shell of ice melted off. They didn't call her the ice witch for nothing. Somehow that cliché had sounded even worse with an English accent.

She'd returned home a wiser woman, she told herself now.

Hurrying to the ancient chest of drawers near the window, she grabbed the brush she'd left there and dragged it through her hair. Then, in a brave moment, she glanced in the mirror before rearing back in horror. Two nights in North Dakota and she looked like this! She'd better keep an eye on the sky or a house would be sure to fall on her. All that would be sticking out was her ruby-colored slippers.

But she didn't care what Tyrel Fox thought of her looks, she reminded herself. All she had to do was get the work done.

She scowled at herself again, brushed her hair back, and bound it with a ribbon.

Maybe she should add a little foundation. A dab of lipstick? A few strokes of mascara.

No! Not for him. Not for the Barbarian Brothers, she determined, and raising her chin, stomped down the stairs to the kitchen.

It was still relatively clean. She found a pan without undue difficulty, switched on the burner with comparative ease, and broke a couple of eggs into a bowl.

Before long she had breakfast cooking. It was still dark outside and the house was quiet. Never in all her twenty-four years had she been up at this hour, or if she had, she'd come at it from the other end.

It was then that she heard the noise. She frowned, glanced into the living room, and saw that Daniel was still asleep beneath his parka.

The sound came again, a scraping, mewling noise. Going to the door, she peeked through the window.

A scrawny cat stared up at her. One ear was half the length of the other, and he held one paw carefully out of the snow. He was the color of swirled marmalade and had an attitude like Sean Connery, well aged but alluring.

Hannah opened the door. "Come on in," she said. "Breakfast is cooking."

The cat entered with wary slowness, watching her the whole while. She noticed now that his tail was truncated barely five inches above his back.

"Cold?"

The cat didn't answer.

"Hungry," she corrected herself, then scowled. What to feed a stray cat in the wee hours of the morning? When she was small, she'd always wanted a cat. But her mother thought them dirty.

This was a cat—kind of, and certainly not too dirty for this place.

"I know just the thing," she said, and smiling, hurried to the kitchen to take the colostrum from the refrigerator.

In a few minutes, Hannah had set a bowl on the kitchen floor, but the cat only looked furtive.

From the living room, she heard Daniel stumble to his feet, so, taking the bowl with her, she went to greet him and set the colostrum there for the cat to eat when he got up the nerve.

"Just a few minutes, Daniel," she said, and pattered back into the kitchen to heat more milk.

She was soon holding a bottle to his mouth.

Daniel stood, arched back, tail lifted as he lowered his charming head and sucked the bottle dry.

"Good boy," Hannah crooned.

Just then the door opened. Ty stepped in. Hannah lifted her gaze, ready to share her success. It was then that all hell broke loose.

Pans clattered. Nate shrieked, a cat yowled, and suddenly the smell of singed fur permeated the house.

Hannah flew into the kitchen only to find a frenzied cat scrambling over the refrigerator and onto the curtain, from which he launched himself, claws spread, over Nate's sprawled body and away.

Ty crossed the living room slowly, his boots squeaking on the floor until finally he leaned his weight against the door-jamb.

"Tell me, Ms. Nelson..."

She turned slowly toward him, fully aware of Nate on the floor, the eggs on Nate, and the pan on the eggs.

"Yes, Mr. Fox?" she said, raising her chin and forcing herself to meet his eyes.

For a moment his gaze skimmed her—the pink cable knit cardigan with the tiny pearl buttons down the front, her hips, her legs, her stocking feet. But then he fastened his attention on her eyes. "Did you come here simply to make my life difficult, or is that just a side benefit?"

She pursed her lips. "As a matter of fact, Mr. Fox, that's my sole purpose in life."

"Really? I'm so flattered."

"As you should be."

"Where'd you find the cat?"

"He found me."

"Your usual type?"

"Better than most I've met."

He snorted. "You're from California then?" he guessed.

"No. Still Colorado, I'm afraid."

"Uh-huh. Nate," he said, turning his attention to his brother who was still on the floor, "we got a calf coming backward."

"I think I broke my tailbone."

"Well, get off it and come help out. She's been at it awhile."

"First calfer?"

"You got it."

"God help us."

"You had breakfast?"

"I watched the eggs fly past my head. That count?"

"You bet. Hannah, I need you to go to town."

"What?" she managed.

"The 4240 won't start. Can't feed without it."

"Forty-two-four-oh?"

"The John Deere. Go to Ellingson's in Valley Green. Tell them I need a new hose."

"Ellingson's?"

"Yeah. Here," he said. Digging around in the overflowing laundry basket, he pulled out a scrap of paper and the stub of a carpenter's pencil. "I'm writing down the number of the part I need. Ellingson'll know what to do. Take the Jimmy."

"Jimmy?"

"My black pickup."

"Pickup?"

"You know how to shift it into four-wheel drive?"

"Four-wheel drive?"

"Did you split a personality with a myna bird or something?" Tyrel asked, scowling at her.

She opened her mouth to speak, but he raised his hand.

"Just...get your coat and I'll show you."

He led the way through the snow to a tan, steel building on the north side of the house. Pushing open a huge, sliding door, he flipped on the lights and made his way between several pieces of huge unidentifiable machinery to a black pickup truck.

"Get in," he said, pulling the door open.

She stepped past him and climbed into the truck. It was built like a tank.

"Shifts just like a car," he said, "only here..." He reached past her to a lever on the floor. His arm brushed her knee. His words stopped.

Her breath stopped. Their gazes met.

"You, um…" He cleared his throat. "You smell pretty good."

For one rash moment she considered apologizing for the eggs, the microwave, the kitchen fire. But then she came to her senses. She raised one brow.

"You smell good, too. For a bull in heat," she said.

He snorted and pulled back. "Honey, bulls don't come in heat. But even if they did, you could freeze 'em up with one flick of your tongue."

"Fiddle dee dee."

"I'd tell you to be careful in town, but I think I'll just issue an all-state warning to the male population. Careful, freezer burn on contact."

She opened her mouth to retaliate, but his face was too close and his eyes as dark as fresh ground coffee. Suddenly she could think of nothing to say.

"How…how do I shift it?" she asked, pulling her gaze away.

"Figure it out," he said, drawing back as if for safety's sake. "You're a smart girl."

Her breath stopped. "I am?" The words came unbidden. Not in two-plus decades of life had anyone ever told her that.

"Yeah, you are," he said. They were staring at each other again. But he ripped his attention away and began digging around in his jeans pocket, came up with a note. "You just *act* like an idiot," he said. "Here. A list of groceries we need. We're going to have to give Daniel a calcium IV if we don't get him milk soon."

She tried to jerk herself back to her senses, but they were still reeling.

He prodded her arm with the list. "You'll find this stuff at a grocery store."

"I know how to buy groceries."

"Well, good. That'll be a first then."

She gritted her teeth. "What do I use for money?"

"Oh. Here." He drew out his billfold and pulled out several twenties. "You're the cook. Get whatever you need."

She raised her brows at him. "A little short for an airline ticket, isn't it? But wait. I've got the *Jimmy*."

His face turned serious. Maybe even a little pale. And as she drove through the brightening day, the memory of his dire expression made her smile.

5

THE TRIP TO VALLEY GREEN was uneventful. Boring, in fact. Hannah flipped on the radio. Country music blasted out at her. Wincing, she trolled for stations. But her only alternatives were the grain futures and a detailed report on the health of the residents of Shady Tree Rest Home. Snapping off the radio, she cruised for a while, but finally switched it on again and let someone named Vince Gill croon at her from a dusty speaker.

Valley Green was neither green nor much of a valley. But Hannah had to admit the white, tree-dotted slopes had a sort of serene beauty. The snow-spattered sign just outside city limits boasted 12,845 people.

Ellingson's Farm Deere and Implement was not hard to find.

Only one employee stood behind the counter. Still in his teens, he was fighting a losing battle against acne and a tendency to let his jaw drop open when he looked at her.

She offered him the smile she used to charm peasants and handed him the note. Still, he didn't focus on the paper.

"I need one of those," she said, tapping the slip.

"Oh. Yes, ma'am," he said, and catapulting back to the business at hand, turned too quickly and ran smack into the wall behind him. Rubber belts of various sizes showered down like acid rain.

After that, things went more smoothly, but then came the grocery store.

Hannah swallowed. Regardless of her words to *Tyrant* Fox, she didn't know the first thing about shopping for groceries.

She could shop for dresses. She was good with shoes. And she was hell on wheels when looking for hats. But *groceries*... That was Maria's department. Or maybe it was Natalie's.

Glancing at the list, Hannah began wandering down a narrow aisle. It wasn't a big store, and yet...

Where did one find peaches? Peaches. She scowled, pattered around and eventually came to a sign extolling the virtues of fresh produce. She regarded the refrigerated shelves. Produce, possibly, she thought. But fresh? Highly unlikely. Picking up one of the smattering of strawberries, she scowled at its faded, wrinkled face before dropping it back down. There was not a peach to be seen. And right now she'd just about die for a papaya. But she supposed she'd have to fly to Hawaii for that. And until she won this current bet, her flying days were through.

"They call these fresh?" said a gravelly voice beside her.

Hannah looked down on a bent head. The woman beside her barely topped four feet tall. Dressed in immaculate white pants and a down coat big enough to protect a Clydesdale from the bitter elements, she raised her face to glare myopically at an orange.

"He calls this a citrus!" complained the tiny woman. "I could grow better oranges on my Christmas cactus." She had a face like a dehydrated apricot.

Hannah didn't even attempt a smile. "Might you know where I could find peaches?" she asked.

"Peaches!" The woman reared back as if zapped by a cattle prod. "Here?" She snorted. "You won't find no peaches here."

Hannah scowled at her list. "I was told to buy peaches."

The old woman scowled. Her features turned from wizened to frightening. "Who told ya?"

Hannah considered that an instant. "A barbarian."

The woman's laugh sounded like a road grader on a bad day, the effects of a cigarette habit cured too late. "A cowboy, huh?"

Now Hannah did smile. The real thing. Straight from the heart. Here was a kindred spirit. "Yes. You might call him that."

"He didn't mean for you to get no fresh peaches. He meant canned."

"They can them?" She shivered. "How awful. Where might I find them?"

The old woman chuckled again. "You're not from around here, huh?"

"No."

Silence as the woman stared up past her bifocals.

"I'm, um…" A lie didn't seem smart, or even safe with a woman like this. "I'm from a lot of places," Hannah said.

"Ahh. What's your name?"

"Hannah." There comes a time when only a lie will do. "Hannah Nelson." She extended her hand, gloved as it was in lambskin cuffed with silver fox. "And you?"

"Mrs. Puttipiece," said the tiny person, reaching out a leathery hand. "Widow Puttipiece. Pansy's my Christian name."

Pansy Puttipiece. She must have really loved her husband to marry into that name. And she'd thought "Hannah Nelson" was bad.

They shook hands. Pansy's grip was as delicate as a road mender's.

"Come on," she said, still carrying the slandered orange.

Hannah followed her slightly bent figure along the dairy section before turning right.

"Here's the canned department."

Hannah gazed in flummoxed wonder. "They have an entire department devoted to abused fruit?"

Pansy chuckled. "You got your Libby's, your Del Monte, your Dole."

"Which is best?"

A shrug. "Canned fruit's all right for Jell-Os and the like. Makes pretty fair muffins. And cowboys can manage to eat 'em straight outta the can. But when I make my tarts and such, I gotta have fresh.''

''You bake fresh tarts?'' She was beginning to salivate like Pavlov's dog. ''By yourself?''

''My Peter— Melvin!'' she barked suddenly.

Beside Hannah, a tall, stooped-shouldered man stopped as if shot. She turned to watch his face turn red, and his paunch disappear as he straightened to face the widow.

''What is it, Mrs. Puttipiece?'' he asked as if pained.

''What is it? It's this thing you call an orange. This ain't no orange. It's a sad excuse. I need my fruits and—''

''Listen here, Mrs. Puttipiece, you can't come in here every day complaining about my produce,'' said Melvin, leaning toward her. ''My oranges is just fine.''

Pansy reared back as if struck. ''At thirty cents apiece. I can't afford no thirty cents on my security check. For thirty cents I could feed caviar to the king of England.''

''It's thirty cents and it'll stay thirty cents!''

''Then I'll be back tomorrow and we can discuss it again,'' she said, stretching up on her toes so that their noses nearly met. ''Since my Peter passed on I got all the time in the world.''

Melvin opened his mouth, gritted his teeth, and said, ''Twenty cents then?''

Settling back on her heels, Pansy nodded. ''That'll do me fine.''

Melvin huffed, then stormed off.

Hannah stood in dumbfounded amazement, then catching Pansy's eye, she said, ''Mrs. Puttipiece, I have a proposition for you.''

Ty PACED AROUND the diameter of the living room one more time. ''Where the hell is she?''

''Don't know,'' said Nate, and strummed a chord on the guitar he was holding cradled on his lap. ''You in a hurry to lose that bet we made?''

''It's past noon. I shouldn't have let her go alone. I should have showed her how to use the four-wheel drive. Dammit! She could be stuck somewhere and freezing to death right now."

"Freezing to death?" Nate struck a G chord and hummed a few notes. "It's twenty-five degrees out there. Near tropical."

"Wearing that little scrap of leather she calls a coat with her head bare and—"

"Shit, Ty, relax," Nathan said. "Keep hyperventilating like that and you're gonna pass out. Hey. That's it. I watch her walk across the room…" he sang. "No, wait. I watch her from across the room. The feelings nearly make me swoon."

"Shut up, Nate."

"Hair as bright as harvest gold," he crooned. "I'd give my very soul to hold—her in my arms for one sweet night. To see her face fill up with light. To feel her sun-kissed satin skin. But I'll not risk my heart again."

"Nathan, shut the hell up!" Tyrel yelled, then, hearing the door open, he swung toward it. "It's about damn time, Hannah.…" he began, then stumbled back a pace as an old woman entered with a bag of groceries.

She was about two feet tall and had a face like a dried apple.

"Hannah," he said, "you shrunk."

"Listen, young man." She glared up at him. "So long as I'm employed here, you'll not be taking the Lord's name in vain."

Tyrel felt his jaw drop, and in that instant Hannah stepped through the doorway.

"Gentlemen," she said, nodding to them. "And I use that term lightly. This is Mrs. Pansy Puttipiece. She's your new housekeeper."

"Housekeeper?" the brothers echoed in harmony.

"And cook," the midget added. "Where's the kitchen?"

"It's in, uh…there," Ty said, motioning lamely.

Puttipiece strode across the cracked linoleum, then stopped in the doorway and raised her brows into her gray, tight-curled hair. "That ain't no kitchen. It's a national disaster. Looks like you got me here just in time."

"It's, uh…it's usually not this bad," Ty said, lying badly.

Pansy snorted, then disappeared into the bowels of the kitchen.

"Um…Miss Nelson, can I talk to you a minute?"

"Certainly, Mr. Fox," Hannah said, meeting his gaze dead-on.

"May I ask you a question?"

"Certainly."

"What the hell do you think you're doing?" he snapped.

"Hey! Watch your language!" roared a voice from the kitchen.

"Yes…yes, ma'am," said Ty, then lowered his voice and tried again. "What the…" He glanced toward the kitchen. "What do you think you're doing?"

"You told me to get whatever I need," she explained, her tone perfectly unruffled. "I got what was needed."

"If I'd just wanted someone to do a little work around the house I got a hundred women who would beg to do the job."

"Really?" Her left brow rose to a surprising height. "The pork queen, maybe?"

"She's a pork princess, and she's not the only one I date."

"Really? Any of them human?"

"You—"

"Ty…Ty," Nate interrupted. "You'd do best to stick to the subject."

Tyrel scowled down at his brother then raised his glare to Hannah. "I can't afford a housekeeper. And even if I could I wouldn't hire *her,*" he whispered. "She's a hundred years old."

Hannah smiled like the proverbial cat. "Believe me, Mr. Fox, she'll do the job I hired her for, and she'll save you money doing it."

"Really!"

"Really."

"And what do *you* plan to do? Sit around and polish your toenails?"

"I don't polish my toenails, Mr. Fox. I buff them. And I believe you hired me to care for your stock."

Exasperated, Ty glanced at his brother. Nate shrugged and strummed a chord. "I never do know what to say," he crooned, "when she looks at me that way. The urge to kiss her—"

"Shut the hell up!"

"Hey!" yelled Pansy.

"Sorry, ma'am," said Ty, then continued, "All right, Ms. Nelson, you want to be just another hand, you'll be just another hand. No more pussyfooting."

"No more pussy," Nate crooned.

"You'll feed stock. You'll clean yards. You'll take your night shifts."

"Whatever you say, *Mr.* Fox," she said.

"Yeah." His anger deflated slightly.

"But I can never stay mad," sang Nate.

"You'll have to have some decent clothes," Ty said. "Here." He led her to the hall closet and dragged out a pair of camel-colored insulated overalls. "They're mine, but they should do the job all right." He almost grinned when he said it, because he was five inches taller and outweighed her by seventy pounds, even when he was doing his own cooking. But, hey, the uglier she looked, the better he'd sleep.

Pushing the overalls into her hands, he stepped back a pace. "You ready to work now, Ms. Nelson?"

"Ready when you are," she said.

And the day began.

BY DARK THEY HAD cleaned the horse barn, fed everything that was breathing and once again bedded the cattle shed.

By seven o'clock Hannah had fed Daniel twice and taken on chores that hadn't been thought of since fall. Still the woman didn't slow down.

She was dressed like a tan snowman. Wearing a man's

billed cap that stuck out from under a faded red hood, she slogged from one job to the next like a bullheaded linebacker.

Ty drooped against the barn doorjamb for a moment, watching as she shoveled out a gate.

"Yeah," Nate said, gazing through the doorway as he passed by with a calf in his arms, "I think you're wearing her down all right. The ice princess on her knees. Pretty soon she'll be kissing your—"

"Shut the hell up, Nate," Ty said. "If I want to know what she'll be kissing, I'll sure enough ask you."

"Well, she sure as hell won't be kissing you."

"You'll see," said Ty.

Nate chuckled, and whistling a tune he called "Old Dogs and Idiots," sauntered off toward the south end of the barn.

By 7:30 Ty thought he would die and half hoped he would.

"Let's call it a night," he said, raising his voice to be heard above the wind.

Hannah looked up from where she was dumping a bucket of grain into the bunk for the bulls. "Already?" she asked, and Ty considered strangling her as he dragged himself off to the house.

Stepping inside, he saw that the entryway was clean.

"You're not planning on wearing them boots in here, are ya?" blasted a voice from the kitchen.

"No, ma'am," he said, and stepping back onto the porch, left his offensive footgear behind.

Hannah and Nate joined him by the time he reached the kitchen. He stopped, let his jaw drop and his taste buds ached.

The place shone like a fresh-scrubbed milking parlor and smelled like culinary heaven.

"What's cooking?" he asked, feeling weak.

"Fried chicken, green beans and baked potatoes."

"How much am I paying you?" Ty asked.

"Six bucks an hour plus free board till I get this place fumigated," she said, looking belligerent.

"If I marry you, will you stay forever?" Nathan asked, looking dreamy.

"There'll be none of that kind of talk!" the widow ordered, but when she turned away, her mouth seemed to have almost turned up. "Sit down."

They did so eagerly. Even Hannah was silent for once, and when the food was delivered all that could be heard was reverent chewing.

Somehow Hannah had become positioned to Ty's left, just inches away. Once the hardest edge of his appetite had been sated, he noticed her proximity like forbidden fruit.

"So..." he said, reaching for a topic to keep his thoughts in line. He had been better off when she was in the overalls, but now that they were removed and her knee was almost touching his, every fiber in him seemed aware of her presence—how her pink sweater hugged her breasts, how her hands moved slowly and precisely when she ate, as if she measured every bite. "Nate," he said, realizing suddenly that he had momentarily forgotten his brother's name. "How're the twins?"

"I'm eating," Nate said, still shoveling potatoes into his mouth.

Ty let him do so for several minutes while he concentrated on his own meal. But suddenly he thought he felt Hannah's knee touch his own. In an instant, she jerked it away.

He refused to look at her. Refused to be drawn into her spider's web.

"Nate!" he said, almost desperate now. "How're the twins?"

"All right," Nate said, devouring a chicken leg. "But the mama can't handle both of 'em. Looks like Hannah'll have herself a new baby to baby—"

Nate's words stopped as he stared at Hannah. Ty scowled, then, unable to avoid her any longer, glanced sideways and realized her face had slumped to the table.

She was sound asleep, her blue eyes closed, her lashes feather soft against her skin.

Tyrel's heart did a twist like a sunfisher bronc coming out of the chute.

"Kinda pretty, ain't she?" Nate said around a mouthful of beans.

Ty glanced at him and his brother smiled, as though even now thinking up a dozen more inane country lyrics to torment him with.

"She's all right in a citified kind of way."

Nate laughed. "Yeah. You gonna carry her to bed or what?"

The sunfisher bronc in Ty's chest stopped cold. "To bed?"

"It'd be the gentlemanly thing to do."

Ty cleared his throat, wiped his damp palms on his jeans and tried not to cry. God, if he touched her he was going to explode.

"Not scared of her, are ya?" Nate asked.

Ty rose with a start. Nate chuckled. Hannah groaned, but didn't awaken.

Easing her chair back, Ty bent and lifted her into his arms. She moaned again, and for a moment all he could think of was that her hair felt like the kittens that were sometimes born in the loft. He could imagine her there, her eyes half-closed as she…

Nate began humming. The sound ripped Ty back into reality. With purposeful strides, he ascended the stairs. Pushing her door open, he strode in and deposited her on the bed.

Her eyes opened, her face only inches from his.

"Mr. Fox?" she said. Her tone was surprised but blurred with sleep.

He cleared his throat and straightened. Diffused light slanted across her bed from the hallway, shadowing and illuminating her lovely face.

"Yeah," he said, wiping his palms on his jeans again. "It's me."

"Oh." Her eyes fluttered shut. "Did I d…"

"What?" he asked, leaning closer.

"Did I do o…"

He sat on the very edge of the bed. "What'd you say?"

"Did I do okay?" she murmured, eyes closed, body lax.

Tyrel's throat tightened. She was asleep, like a little girl who had slaved to please a father who would never be pleased.

"Yeah, honey," he said, sweeping a few strands of hair from her forehead. "Yeah. You did perfect."

HANNAH AWOKE just after 6:00. Her body throbbed like a digital sound system. But she'd managed to feed Daniel twice during the night before falling into oblivion again. Now, despite the aches, the scrapes and her grumbling stomach—probably due to the fact that she'd fallen asleep in her dinner—she felt strangely elated.

Stumbling her way to the bathroom, she took a quick shower. The curtain had been replaced and the toilet cleaned, she noticed. Beneath the warm stream of heavenly water, she lathered her body and sang a few bars of something she'd heard yesterday, then felt embarrassed about the silly lyrics and tried to remember a little Pavarotti.

Twenty minutes later she was dressed in jeans and a blue mohair sweater, and went down the stairs.

Delectable aromas wafted to her. The Fox boys sat at the kitchen table.

"Good morning," she said.

The brothers looked up.

"Morning," Nate responded.

Ty made a strangled noise above his coffee cup.

Nate grinned. "Ty'd say good morning too, but he swallowed his tongue. Say good morning, Ty."

"Shut up, Nate," he mumbled, and shifted his gaze to his coffee.

"You look especially nice this morning, Hannah," Nate said, still grinning. "That sweater brings out the color of your eyes. Don't it bring out the color of her eyes, brother?" he asked, nudging Ty.

Tyrel looked up, and suddenly it didn't matter that she was a Clifton Vandegard or that her father was one of the most influential men in LA, because Tyrel's eyes were dark and entrancing, drawing at something deep in her soul.

There were light crinkles at the corner of his eyes and his mouth was full and sensual, as if it could soothe a spooked horse and croon Shakespeare at the same time.

"Amy'd look good in a sweater like that," Nate said. "Where'd you get it?"

Reality flashed back in.

Hannah blushed and hurried to take her seat. "Um...Paris," she said.

Silence filled the room, broken only by the sound of bacon frying. All eyes turned to her.

"I, uh...I had a chance to visit there once."

"Ahhh," Nate said, swallowing a half a glass of milk.

Pansy, busy at the stove, began dishing up breakfast and setting plates in front of them.

Hannah stared at hers. Three eggs, a couple strips of bacon, two pieces of buttered toast and a sliced orange. More food than she had consumed in all of 1997. "Wow," she said.

"Yeah," sighed Nate.

"Eat up," ordered Pansy, her spatula held like a whip.

Hannah ate her orange first. True, she was hungry, but no one loved a fat woman. Her mother's words were still very clear on that.

Despite the slathering of butter, she ate the toast. It tasted comparable, maybe even superior, to Spago's cream-cheese croissants. The milk was almost yellow with fat and icy cold.

She pushed her plate away.

Pansy turned from the stove like a sergeant at the sound of shelling. "What do you think you're doing?"

"It was delectable," Hannah said. "But I couldn't eat another bite."

They were all looking at her again as if she were extraterrestrial.

"Really," she said. Glancing at them all in turn, she laughed nervously. "I have to watch my weight or I won't fit into my...uniform...thingies."

"Yeah," Nate said. "That's a worry."

"You gotta eat," Ty said, watching her solemnly.

She laughed again. The sound of his whiskey-rough voice did strange things to her insides, and the somber concern in his eyes was about to melt the fifty-dollar-an-ounce moisturizer right off her face.

"I'm a big girl now," she said, laughing again. From the corner of her eye, she noticed that Daniel had wandered into the doorway. "I've been deciding what to eat for quite some time."

"I don't want you fainting out there. We've got a full day ahead of us, you know," Ty said, "and—"

"And you want to get your money's worth?" she asked. Daddy had once said her temper could rise faster than a superstar's ego.

"I sure—"

"Hey!" interrupted Pansy, bristly brows pressed tight over the plastic frames of her bifocals. "I don't take no arguing over my meals. And anyhow, I got something to say."

"Yes, ma'am?"

All three of them spoke at once.

"It's *him!*" Pansy said, pointing her spatula at the little Angus. "He's gotta go."

"Daniel Day-Lewis?"

Tyrel watched Hannah's eyes widen in horror, and wished for the hundredth time that he could keep his head straight when she was around. Never once had he said the right thing.

"I don't care if he's Lewis or Errol Flynn or Valentino. He ain't staying in my house."

"But..." Hannah stumbled to her feet. "He'll die outside."

"He's a cow," Pansy said.

"He's not. He's just a calf. All alone. A baby. Isn't he, Ty?"

When she turned toward him, Ty felt as if she'd shredded his heart into a million tiny strips. He could do nothing but nod.

"And he can't go out," Hannah murmured.

"It's him or me," Pansy said.

Ty rose to his feet. "He *is* a baby, Hannah, but he's doing real good."

Their eyes met. Hers were as blue and wide as a summer sky, but they shone with liquid brightness in the harsh overhead light. He wondered frantically if she might cry. His lacerated heart ached.

"He's doing real good 'cuz of you, honey," he said.

"Really?" The single word was soft.

"Sure. But, um…but he's from my best heifer, you know. I'm hoping to keep him for breeding."

"So you wouldn't have to sell him?"

"Hell, no!"

Pansy cleared her throat, but he didn't notice. God in heaven, Hannah was beautiful.

"Hell, no," he said again. "He'll be a show bull like Houdini. We'll keep him till he's old as Methuselah and can't do nothing but gnaw grain with the heifers, but only if he learns that he's a bull and not a…a house cat."

Her bottom lip was trembling. Oh, God. He was going to take her in his arms and then heaven help his heart.

Nate hummed.

Ty tightened his fists and remained resolutely where he was. "He's gotta go out, Hannah," he said.

"But how'll I feed him at night?"

"She's been feeding him at night?" Nate asked.

"Every three hours," Ty said, then shuffled his feet. "I, uh…I noticed. And I appreciate it, Hannah. But you don't need to worry. He'll be fine out there. We got a little pen on the south side of the barn. We'll bed it down good. When the weather's nice he can lay in the sun, and when it's bad he can scamper in under the roof. It's just like a…just like a spa," he said.

Her fists were tightened, and for one wild second he wanted nothing more than to kiss her until they fell open and she would relax and unfold like a hothouse flower in his hands.

He would kiss her until she was breathless, love her like she
needed to be loved.

"Really?" she whispered.

"Yeah." He swallowed hard. "Really."

6

THEY LEFT DANIEL in the living room while they bedded the little calf pen together. The sun was out today and as she worked, it warmed her face.

She still felt choked up about moving Daniel from the house, but this was a nice spot with the sun slanting past the lean-to to fall on the bright yellow straw that they'd spread twelve inches deep for his bed.

"Looks like spring might finally come after all," Tyrel said.

She didn't respond. She'd acted like a fool in the kitchen and felt silly about it now. After all, he was just a calf, not like her next of kin or something. Still, he was all alone with no mother. Not even a dad to love him in that proud, distracted way she could never understand.

"He's going to be all right, Hannah."

She turned toward him. Tears filled her eyes.

From the elm by the tack room a robin trilled.

Ty cleared his throat, but his voice was still raspy when he spoke. "Really, Hannah, if you cry I'm going to have to kiss you, and then all hell's going to break loose, 'cuz I don't even know who you are. Or how long you're stayin'."

"I just…" She gathered her wits, and stumbled back a step. "I'm sorry," she said, and fled to the house.

TY LOITERED AROUND the porch for a half an hour, trying to forget the image of her eyes, her face, stricken with some sorrow far deeper than ejecting a bull calf from a living room.

The cows needed feeding, the heifers checking, and for the life of him, he couldn't force himself to do either.

"What're you doing?" Nate called from the barn.

Ty glanced up, irritable and fidgety. "None of your damn business."

Nate laughed out loud, hummed a few notes and ducked back into the barn.

It was then the door opened. Ty turned back, and there on the porch, stood Hannah. The little Angus was in her arms, his broad, wedge-shaped head peeking out from beneath the parka.

"You okay?" Ty asked. It was a stupid question, of course, but it was the best he could do on such short notice. He'd only had thirty minutes or so to think up that line.

"Yes. I'm fine."

She descended the stairs like a princess carrying the crown jewels.

"I can carry him for you."

"No...thank you. He's not heavy."

Her voice broke on the last word. Dear God, why did he fall for this kind of woman? Why not Mary Ann or Roxanne or Shelly. Shelly loved him. She'd said as much. And she was solid, bred for farm life, and a kindhearted woman.

But this woman... She wasn't kind. She was snooty. But when he glanced into her eyes, he called himself a liar.

He pushed the barn door open for her. She passed him quickly, and in a minute was bending to set Daniel on his feet. Reluctantly she pulled the parka off him.

Ty raised his brows. A pink cardigan covered his back. The sleeves encased his sturdy, black legs, and along his belly, each little pearl button was fastened.

"That sweater out of fashion?" he asked.

"I got it in London."

She stared at the calf. He stared at her.

"I never much cared for England," she said.

Ty knew he should keep quiet. He also knew, somehow,

with that extra sense that men weren't supposed to have, that her memories had something to do with a man.

"How do you feel about Englishmen?" he asked.

She sighed. "They're jerks."

"Yeah?" He couldn't help the fact that his tone had lost its tension.

She looked at him. His breath stopped.

"Yeah," she said.

"Well." His pulled his gaze away from her with an effort. "Daniel looks damn fine in that sweater. Pink's his color."

She smiled. He couldn't help but notice. It was like the crack of a rosy dawn and drew his attention like a beacon.

"He'll really be okay?"

He'd never really seen her smile, not like this—tremulous, real, as if they were buddies, and more....

"Ty?"

"Huh?"

"I said, he'll be okay?"

"Oh, yeah! Hell." Geez, he was acting like an idiot. "Come here," he said, stepping from the pen.

She followed him back into the interior of the barn.

They stood between two rows of open stalls. Each of them contained a cow and a calf. He led her to the last one, opened a gate and motioned her inside.

"Come on in. She won't hurt you. These Angus, they're supposed to be spooky, but we all but hand-feed 'em. After a while they settle down. Good thing, too, 'cuz we'd lose more than we do if they were as wild as the roping steers. Twins don't always make it."

"Twins?" she said, but just then the second calf peeked around its mother's tail.

The calves were small, identical, adorable, even to Tyrel, and he had seen his share.

"Yeah, twins. But she won't be able to keep 'em both."

"What?" Hannah's eyes were already wide in horror.

"No! They won't die!" he hurried to explain. "Not

if…you know, not if the good Lord's willing. But she's a first-calf heifer. Not enough milk for them both.''

She scowled slightly, barely drawing a line in her fine brow. ''What'll you do with them?''

''We'll bottle-feed one. Put him in with Daniel. So he'll have a friend. In fact, we could do that right now…if it would make you feel better.''

She smiled again, that strange, timid expression that seemed to have seen too little of the light of day. ''No,'' she said, pulling her gaze away from him and moving nervously back through the gate. ''It's okay, if you're sure he'll be all right.''

He meant to close the gate, but her gaze was on him again, muddling his senses. The gate swung toward him, bumping him in the back.

She laughed and reached for it just as he did the same.

Their hands brushed, their breath held. They faced each other like two startled cats, nervous and wary.

''Yeah,'' he said. ''Yeah. Everything'll be just fine.''

THE DAYS PASSED like water through a sieve. Hannah learned a hundred things she never thought she'd want to know.

Daniel began filling out and was soon accompanied by the smallest of the twins who was given into Hannah's care and dubbed Roony.

Sean, the cat, chose Hannah's bed to hide under during the day. Because of that and Pansy's obvious irritation over a hairy beast in ''her'' house, Hannah moved his litter box into her room and kept the door closed until night, when she left it open a smidgen so he could prowl the interior like the great white hunter.

Pansy, either because of her frenetic cleaning or the clarity of her conscience, slept like the proverbial dead and didn't realize his nocturnal adventures.

Nearly a week had passed when the thermometer rose to forty astounding degrees. Snow melted in earnest. It trickled from the huge mounds that had been piled everywhere and hastened down to the stream that wound its way through the cow pastures.

At noon, Hannah joined the others in the kitchen. The smell of hot chili filled her nostrils, and she smiled as Pansy handed her a bowl.

"So, Nate," Ty said, "you busy today?"

"Nope," Nate replied, already crumbling a gargantuan mound of crackers over his chili. "Thought I'd have me a long bubble bath then put my feet up and maybe watch my soaps."

Ty snorted. "I meant tonight."

Nate shook his head once as if Ty were daft. "It's Saturday night, brother."

"Damn. Again?"

"They come round every seven days or so."

Hannah hid a grin around her spoon. It was like Ty to neither know nor care what day of the week it was.

"So you're playing at the Roughhouse?" Ty asked.

"Me and the Restless Cowboys. Have been for the past year and a half." There was a pause as Nate closed his eyes and dissected every individual flavor of the meal. "Have I asked you to marry me yet, Pansy?"

"Every day since I been here."

"Have you accepted?"

"Do I look desperate to you?" she asked, turning her dried-apple face to him and brandishing a wooden spoon. "Now you eat up. All of you. You're like three walking skeletons. Don't know why I waste my time on you."

Nate chuckled. Ty grinned.

Hannah felt a strange contentment settle over her.

"What'd you have in mind?" Nate asked.

"'Bout time to get them roping horses fit. If they're half so out of shape as me, it's gonna take a good month of Sundays to get the kinks out."

Out of shape. Hannah allowed herself one quick glance at Ty. He looked about as out of shape as a gymnast primed for the Olympics. He turned toward her, catching her gaze. She hastened hers back to her meal.

"Rowdy don't get kinks," Nate said. "He's like a da…"

"Hey!" barked Pansy. She had an uncanny way of sensing an impending swearword, like a hound before an earthquake.

"Sorry," Nate said, already filling his bowl with seconds. "Rowdy's like a machine."

"I'm thinking of using Maverick," Ty said, sipping his coffee.

"Maverick! Geez! Is there some reason you don't want to make money at this roping gig?"

"Maverick's got the stuff," Ty argued, sounding defensive.

"Maverick's scared of cows."

Ty scowled. "He ain't scared."

"So he just bolted and left you lying there in the mud last spring for kicks and grins."

"He's Hazard's best gelding."

"Yeah, well, you find some other way to promote your stallion's genes, 'cuz old Maverick ain't gonna cut the mustard."

Ty glared into his coffee cup. "Lot you know," he grumbled, but he seemed unable to argue the point.

"Which one is Maverick?" Hannah inquired.

"You telling me old Ty ain't showed him to you yet?" Nate asked, glancing at his brother. "He's been extolling that gelding's virtues for four years. 'Look at them lines. Look at that headset. See how he travels. Endless potential.' Ain't that right, Ty?"

"That's right," Ty said, still grumpy, then cleared his throat and glanced at Hannah. "He's the big brown one out back of the barn."

"Legs like stilts, brain like rocks. You can't miss him," said Nate.

"The blood bay?" Hannah asked.

"Yeah."

"He must be seventeen hands tall," she said, remembering

the horse. He stood out like an ostrich among banty hens, all legs and neck and big soft eyes.

"Damn near— Sorry," Ty said, automatically glancing at Pansy, but not losing his enthusiasm. "Darn near seventeen hands," he said. "Hazard can throw the size."

"He's got a tiny head for a big horse like that," Hannah said.

"Yeah. If there's one thing Hazard puts on 'em it's a wide brow and those big old eyes."

Unable to help herself, Hannah smiled. Tyrel Fox was like a boy in a candy shop when it came to his horses.

"I, uh," he said, seeming embarrassed by his fervor. "Tonight after chores I could show you Hazard's other babies. You could see how he crosses with the mares we got." There was a pause. "If you like."

She felt like a teenager, lost for words and drowning in her own hormones. "Okay," she said.

"I'm gonna need to go home." Pansy glanced from Ty to Hannah and back. "Tonight. I need someone to give me a ride."

"You're coming back, aren't you?" Nate's tone was fairly panicked. He stopped the ladle in midair just about to dump another load of chili into his bowl. There were few who loved food more than Nathan Fox, Hannah thought, and wondered now if that appetite would ever catch up to him. So far, he was just as lean and hard as his brother.

Pansy frowned at him. "Course I'm coming back. You think I'd leave you three to fend for yourselves. Wouldn't be Christian. 'Fraid you might turn to cannibalism or something."

"Phew!" Nate put his hand to his heart. "I was afraid I was going to have to move back home. Dad's heavy-handed as a drill sergeant, but at least Mom can cook up a decent meal." He stopped suddenly. "No offense, Hannah. When are you coming back, Pansy?"

"I need me some time off, too," she groused. "Can't work all the time."

The room was silent.

"I'll be back after church."

Hannah stifled her grin. Everyone needed to be needed. It was a lesson she had just learned. And apparently no one needed to be needed more than Pansy Puttipiece.

In the end, it was decided that the widow would stay home in Valley Green until Monday morning, and then would drive her own car to The Lone Oak.

Hannah returned to work. The sun was warmer still today. On the hillside, the calves were bellowing as they cavorted about. Their mothers chewed their cuds and watched them with big, prideful eyes.

In his corral alone, Hazard, the quarter horse stallion, paced and called to his harem.

The mares, pregnant and round-bellied, looked back with expressions ranging from boredom to disdain.

Hannah laughed as she called the broodmares into their stalls.

"Poor Hazard," Ty said from behind her.

Hannah caught her breath and turned. He was standing in the doorway. He must be the most hot-blooded creature on earth, she thought, because he'd removed his jacket and rolled up the sleeves of his chambray shirt. His wrists were broad and sprinkled with dark hair, his low-brimmed hat pushed back on his head.

"He doesn't get much attention," he continued, nodding toward the stallion as the mares rushed back to their stalls.

"Maybe the girls will show more interest after they drop their foals," Hannah said, searching for conversation. His proximity did evil things to her blood pressure.

"Let's hope so." Ty slid the door shut behind a sorrel mare. "It's gotta be hard on his ego. Talking dirty to 'em every day like that and they don't even prick up an ear."

She shouldn't enter this conversation and she knew it, but his voice was low and smoky, reeling her in. "Is that what he's doing?" she asked. "Talking dirty?"

"Yeah." There was a pause as the last door closed. "Want to know what he says?"

She turned to face him. Her breath stopped.

The barn was silent, but for horses munching.

"Sorry." He pulled his gaze quickly away. "Sorry. I didn't…" He let out a heavy sigh. "I don't know what I'm thinking sometimes." Silence. "I was just wondering if you might want to go for a ride."

"On a horse?"

She looked so surprised that he couldn't help but chuckle. "I guess I've been working you pretty hard, huh?"

"Have you?" she asked, and smiled. "I didn't notice."

"I suppose you always work like this," he said.

"Me. No. Just when I'm on vacation."

"Really?"

"Sure."

He leaned against Tuff Tina's stall and bent one knee to rest the bottom of his boot on the plank behind him.

"So you on vacation now?" he asked.

"You might say that."

It was foolish, he knew, but for a moment it almost seemed she was serious. He tried to keep his head. "So would a ride ruin your sabbatical?"

"No." She shook her head. "A ride would be nice."

Behind the barn were the unpampered horses. They were also some of The Lone Oak's best stock. Skippa Lula, the palomino mare Nate used for roping, was the most dependable.

Ty slipped a halter over her head and handed the lead rope to Hannah. Then he haltered the chestnut he'd used for heeling for the past five years.

Back inside the barn, Ty tied Rowdy near a stall and motioned Hannah down the aisle a ways.

"Cross ties are there," he said. He watched as she moved forward and quickly snapped a rope into each side of Lula's halter. Whatever Hannah Nelson was or wasn't, she knew horses.

Inside the tack room, he lifted a chocolate-colored saddle from a rack. "This all right for you?" he asked. "It's the smallest I've got."

"Ahh…" She looked baffled for a moment, then said, "Sure. That's fine."

"Okay. Grab that blanket and the hackamore hanging there," he said, and moved back into the aisle.

Hannah placed the blanket on the mare's back without prompting. Ty sat the saddle atop it.

"Can you cinch up while I see to Rowdy?"

She blinked at him. She'd shed her overalls for a goose-down jacket that Howard had left behind. It was faded, out of date, ripped on one sleeve and generally ugly. Funny how she still looked like a princess in it. Even the tattered, tweed cap he'd offered her, made her look adorable, like royalty incognito, with soft hair and fire in her eyes.

"Sure," she said finally. "I can, uh…cinch up."

"Okay." His own roping saddle was high pommeled. Over the years he'd grown accustomed to the feel of it and used it all the time now. It took him only a few minutes to tighten the girth, slip a bit between Rowdy's teeth and turn toward Hannah.

She was standing with one stirrup draped over the seat of the saddle as she stared in bewilderment at the string girth.

So she was an English rider and didn't know how to cinch up a Western saddle. It was as plain as the nose on Ty's face. There were a thousand remarks he could make about that. Instead, he led his gelding up beside the mare and handed his reins to Hannah.

"Here you go. Let me do that. Put your gloves on before your fingers stiffen up."

She did so.

In a minute they were out of the barn and riding down the gravel road.

So who was she? Ty wondered for the hundredth time. Where was she from and what was she doing here?

He didn't voice the questions.

Off to his right a trio of robins hopped about, looking puffy and disgruntled in the snow.

Hannah turned toward them, seeming to ride without conscious thought.

"Dammit, Frank," Ty said, raising his voice to an odd birdlike falsetto. "I told you it was too early to come back here. We should have stayed in Florida."

To his surprise, Hannah laughed. His heart flip-flopped in his chest.

The rest of the ride was filled with talk and laughter. He showed her where, at the top of a distant rise, they could just see the trees that surrounded his parents' house.

To the west, in a ravine where a bunch of scrubby box elders grew was where he had found a wounded fawn as a child. He'd carried it home and kept it until it lost its spots and moved on. But sometimes he thought he still caught glimpses of it.

Hannah watched him as he talked. Sometimes she turned away to gaze at the widespread country around them, and ask all sorts of questions.

What kind of bird? Had he always wanted to be a rancher? How many foals was he expecting? And with each of her questions, Ty's own life seemed to take on a new significance, a new glow.

Finally the sun sunk beneath the low, western hills, casting midnight blue shadows across the snow. They reached the barn just as the last glimmer of light faded.

Supper was nothing more than a continuation of the same mood. Nate, eager for an evening with his band, was at his comical best. Even Pansy cracked what might be referred to as a smile.

Finally the meal was over and Nate and Pansy were gone for the night.

"Well..." Ty shuffled his feet, feeling suddenly nervous. He'd gotten somewhat accustomed to Hannah's regal beauty, could almost breathe evenly in her presence now. But that was with others about. Now, alone with her, he felt his heart rate pick up and his temperature rise. "I guess I'll go check the heifers. That'll give me till midnight or so before I have to do it again."

Hannah turned toward him. She'd spent the past hour or so upstairs while he'd padded about the lower floor trying not to image what she was doing up there. But it had been hopeless. She had taken a bath. He'd heard the water running, knew when it had been turned off, sensed the whisper of her blouse as she'd slipped it from her body. Almost *felt* the lap of the soft waves as she'd stepped into the tub.

"I'll go out at midnight for you," she said.

She was wearing a soft salmon-colored sweater tucked into her jeans. It caressed her breasts, accentuated her tiny waist and made his mouth go dry.

"Ty."

"Huh?" He snapped out of his reverie, feeling patently stupid, and ridiculously overheated.

"I said I'll check them at midnight."

"No. That's all right," he said. It was going to be hard enough to sleep knowing they were the only two in the house. If he had to worry about her out there all alone, he might just as well kiss his poor lonely bed goodbye. "I *want* to go out."

She stared at him as if he'd lost his mind. And maybe he had.

"No, really. The cold air will do me good." Never was a truer word spoken. The March night air was just about as effective as a brisk shower.

"You can't expect to do your part and Nate's."

"He'll be home by..." Ty shrugged. "Five or so."

"In the morning?"

"Yeah. So that just leaves me three trips out there before breakfast." He grinned. It sounded ridiculously masochistic when he said it that way.

"Then I'm going out."

He tried to dissuade her, but it was no use. Finally, dressed for the elements, they wandered out side by side. He justified this by telling himself that if she was going to take up the night watch, he'd have to show her what to look for.

The night was very still and very bright. The sky was clear with a three-quarters moon that shone on the melting snow like a huge chandelier.

Hannah drew the chill air deep into her lungs. There was a freshness here she had never before experienced. A peace, an acceptance. She shivered, filled with emotions she neither understood nor wished to analyze.

"You cold?"

"No." She glanced at Ty, then shifted her gaze from his shadowed face to the pastures that fell away before them. "It's very pretty here," she said softly.

"Prettier than Boston?"

She turned back and raised her brows to stare into his downturned face. "I'm from Colorado," she said.

He laughed. The sound shivered through her. "Oh, yeah. Here," he said. Lifting one strand of barbed wire in a bare hand, he pressed the other down with his foot so she could scoot between them. "Watch your head."

In a moment they were on the other side, but he stopped her now with a hand on her arm. Taking off her tweed cap, he unfolded the flap and placed it back on her head. "You gotta keep your ears covered," he said. Their gazes met. Softness swirled around them.

But in an instant Ty cleared his throat and turned away.

"Didn't your mom teach you anything?"

They walked side by side through the darkness, their hands shoved deep into their pockets. "Tell me, Tyrel Fox, are you always such a mother hen?" she asked.

He looked straight ahead. Fog rose in cool clouds in the dip before them. "Have you ever noticed that you evade every question I ask you?"

"I do not."

"Yes, you do."

Through the fog, she could see clusters of cows lying on the snow-covered hills ahead of them. "Wouldn't it be wiser to keep the cows inside if you know they're going to deliver soon?''

''There's not enough room for all of them. If we know they're due we separate them and put them in the barn with the newborns. But they can be unpredictable, and you're changing the subject again.''

''I am not.''

''The subject was your mother.''

''Speaking of mothers, when are your mares due?''

He stopped in his tracks and faced her. ''You know my brother, my occupation, my address, my...'' He paused, searching for more words. ''Dammit, Hannah, you know everything but my hat size. Don't you think you could trust me with...hell, I don't know, your middle name or something?''

No, she couldn't. But his voice had gone all soft and smoky again, curling in her insides. She looked away.

''It's Ann.''

''Really?''

She grinned at the surprise in his tone. ''What else would you like to know?''

The night was very quiet. Not a car, not a plane, not a whisper of wind could be heard.

''Anything,'' he murmured. ''Just give me anything.''

She turned back to him and felt her senses scramble. Beneath the shadow of his hat brim, his jaw looked as rugged and real as the land around them.

She jerked her gaze away, walking toward the herd again. In a few strides he caught up with her.

''She taught me which spoon to use for sorbet,'' Hannah said.

''What?'' He pulled her to a halt with a hand on her arm.

''That's what Mother taught me,'' she said, her voice almost inaudible to her own ears.

The moon was at his back and shone full on her face.

''Do you look like her?'' he asked softly, unable, for all his self-warning, to keep from touching her cheek, to stop himself from pushing a few golden strands behind her ear.

She shivered beneath his touch. "Too big boned," she said.

"What?"

She drew a soft breath between her lips. They were beautiful lips, perfect, pink as evening clouds. "Mother was very refined," she added.

"Was?" He realized suddenly that he was holding his breath.

"She died in a car accident when I was..." She stopped as if somehow this delicate information might be used against her. "Quite young," she finished softly.

He touched her cheek again, wishing with all his aching heart that he could pull her into his arms, could ease the pain he saw in her face and knew she would never admit to. But he had no right to share her emotions.

"I'm sorry," he said.

She glanced over his left shoulder. "I didn't see her much anyway."

"And your father?"

"He travels a good deal."

The night was quiet.

"Didn't they know?" he murmured.

She stared at him with eyes wide beneath the tattered tweed. "What?" she asked. It seemed as if she tried to contain the question, but it crept out on a feather-soft whisper.

He should stop. Should turn away. Should send her back to wherever she came from. Should have learned long ago not to give a woman like this a rope to hang him with.

"Didn't they know how precious you are?" he asked.

He waited for her rejoinder, her admittance that she was indeed worth her weight in gold.

But in an instant, he realized that her eyes were too bright and her perfect lips trembling. He searched for words, but his throat was tight, and his mind jumbled by her softness, her beauty, her vulnerability that ripped at his soul.

"Thank you." Her words were so small he could barely hear them.

Closing his eyes, he shushed all the warning bells and wrapped her in his embrace. It took a moment, but finally she lifted her arms and hugged him back.

And so they stood with the moon shining bright and hopeful upon them, doing nothing but holding each other. Yet it felt like so much more, like the completion of a dream, like coming home after a long journey.

Finally she stirred in his arms and moved away slightly.

He heard her clear her throat, and watched her glance nervously to the right, as if letting down her guard was such a horrid thing that she could not even face him.

"You all right?" He should have thought of something clever to say, but couldn't.

"Yes," she said. The word was soft, but instead of looking away, she raised her gaze to his, and smiled. He smiled back. "I'm good," she said.

He tried to let her go, tried to let her draw away, but he could not, not completely, not now. And so he tucked her hand under his elbow.

Arm in arm, they walked through the darkness. The cows lay content and quiet, chewing their cuds, barely glancing up as they strolled by. Ty pointed out certain animals and their various attributes. Even in the dark, he knew them, their family, their history. As if they were old friends. Geez, he needed to get a life, he thought. But with her there beside him it seemed like more happiness than he could bear. Certainly too much to keep.

"And that one there..." He pointed to his right, where a black heifer lay alone. "That's Cranky II."

"You have them named?"

He smiled down at her. "Just a few. Those that bear remembering. Her mother was the meanest damn cow I ever saw. I was, oh, maybe fifteen when Dad got her. Bought her at an auction with twenty or so others. We had a girl neighbor—Elaine Anderson." He said the name reverently, then sighed. "I thought she was the prettiest thing that ever walked on two legs."

She was staring at him.

"Buck teeth didn't bother me back then," he said. "And that hook nose—it only added to her beauty." Hannah's laughter trickled to his soul. "Anyway, she'd come over with her dad to see the new stock. And me, I thought this was my chance to strut my stuff." He winced. "I told you I was only fifteen, didn't I?"

Funny. Every time she smiled, a knot formed in the pit of his stomach. Right about now he had a pile of them that'd make a sailor proud.

"You told me," she said, music in her voice.

"Anyway, I ducked through the fence and walked on into the herd, real cockylike, a cattleman looking over his domain, you know. Checking this one's hooves, that one's legs." He shook his head. "I never saw the old bat coming. She hit me like a two-ton truck and rolled me like a sausage. By the time Dad chased her off me I felt like I'd been mauled by a bear."

"Oh, no," Hannah said, but her voice cracked when she said it.

"Oh, yes," he disagreed. "But the worst part was when I looked up, there was Elaine, doubled over, laughing her head off."

"Oh, no," she repeated.

"You wouldn't do that, would you?" he asked, leaning close to gaze into her face. "You wouldn't laugh at my misfortune."

"No," she said, and burst into openmouthed laughter.

He watched her until she was done and the noise had turned to chuckles. Then he tucked her arm beneath his own and headed toward the barn.

"You're an evil woman, Hannah Nelson," he said.

"I know." She dabbed at her eyes. "I'm sorry."

He chuckled because it didn't sound as though she was sorry at all.

"But I'll make it up to you."

"Yeah?" He couldn't help his breathless tone. "How?"

She glanced away, nervous again. "I'll take two watches tonight."

"That wasn't quite what I was hoping for," he admitted, and led her into the yard to check the cows most likely to deliver before dawn.

When he switched on the overhead lights, the cows blinked. Near the far wall, a black heifer rose nervously to her feet. He knew immediately that something was up.

"Looks like we got us some action," he said softly.

"How can you tell?"

He nodded toward the heifer. "See how she's standing—hind legs spread. Looks flighty. It's her first calf. It spooks them sometimes. And see, she's sweating."

"What do we do?" Her words were breathy.

Normally, he might rope her, do an exam, chase her in with the newborns. But the night was so warm and friendly, and with Hannah at his side, those options seemed patently unappealing.

"I like to let them handle it themselves if possible. And I'm not going to get any sleep now until I know the outcome here. We could just hunker down in the straw over there, kind of out of sight, and watch and wait."

He'd used the wrong vernacular. He remembered the day she'd arrived. She wasn't the hunkering kind, she'd said. He waited for her to say it again.

"All right," she said instead.

Finding a spot half-hidden behind a cluster of cows, they sat, their backs against the wall of the shed, their bottoms sunk into the sweet, clean bedding of straw.

"So this is how you spend your Saturday nights?" she asked.

He looked at her. She was a narrow, sexy slice of dark heaven only inches away. "They're generally not this exciting."

She laughed. The sound melted its way into his already punch-happy heart.

"How 'bout you?" he asked.

"Me?" She sounded surprised but only slightly wary. "Same with me."

He snorted, but she held his gaze.

"Usually not so exciting," she said.

Well, geez, there really wasn't any hope for it. He had to touch her.

The straw rustled as he leaned toward her. Beneath his fingers, her face felt as soft as a dream. "You're not playing by the rules," he said.

He watched her swallow. "No?" The word sounded tense.

"You're supposed to say something nasty."

"I, uh…" She was holding her breath. "I can't think of anything. Sorry."

"I'll forgive you," he murmured, and touched his lips to hers.

It was only supposed to be a touch, a moment. But she kissed him back, hesitant and shy, slanting across his lips like a taste of Eden. The sweetness of it shocked him, thrilled him, pulled at him like the call of the wild. He wanted to drag her into his arms and carry her to bed.

He drew back, breathing hard. "Wow!" It was the best he could come up with.

She pulled her lower lip between her teeth. "Wow?" she echoed. And in that word there were a thousand emotions.

"Yeah," he said. "Wow."

Was he teasing her? she wondered wildly. Did he, like Derik, think she was an ice queen? If there was one thing she couldn't stand, it was to be made fun of. If men thought her cold, then cold she would be, and far too good for the likes of them.

But now she couldn't stand the thought. Not when *his* touch seemed as warm as the summer sun, as wondrous and alluring as magic. Even now she felt herself drawn toward him. And suddenly their lips were touching again. Her heart clipped along like running hooves in her chest and every nerve ending throbbed with sensation.

But what did he feel?

"Hannah, I..." He drew back, breathing hard, and reaching out, he touched her cheek.

She closed her eyes to the feelings. He slid his fingers, slow as forever, along her jaw and down her throat. It was only then that she realized his hand was trembling.

7

TYREL DREW BACK and caught her gaze. "Hannah?"

Her breath came in soft pants. It no longer mattered that they were worlds apart, for the feelings that soared through her were all consuming, making her head spin and her heart sing. "Yes?"

"There is no gal in town."

"What?"

"Shelly," he explained, his words fragmented and his eyes intense. "We broke up six months ago or so."

"Yes?"

"Yeah. It seems she could think of more exciting things to do on a Saturday night."

"More exciting than this?" She didn't even try to keep the honesty from her tone.

He smiled. Her heart tripped. "Shelly would have made a fine wife but there wasn't…" He paused and ran the backs of his fingers down her throat. She shivered at the touch. "There was never the fire, the feelings that you need to make forever last. Not like…" He stopped his words and drew his hand slowly away to curl it into a loose fist. Turning his gaze aside, he said, "Looks like she's down again."

"What?"

He cleared his throat. "The heifer. She's been down on the other side of those cows. Maybe we better take a look."

Taking her hand in his own, he pulled her to her feet, then, quiet and slow, they skirted the wall until he pulled her back down to a squatting position where he raised his arm and pointed.

"See." His voice was soft. "The front feet and the nose are out."

Hannah spotted the heifer. She was lying flat-out on her side, and straining. The feet and nose Ty had mentioned, didn't look like feet and a nose at all, but rather like a purple-veined plastic bag with something bumpy trapped inside and trying to get out. But as the heifer strained again, the legs emerged a bit more. The placenta was pushed back, so that Hannah could now see a shiny black head pressed flat against forelegs. Once the head was free the body came in a rush, slippery and wet and the most spectacular process Hannah had ever witnessed in real life.

She stared in openmouthed amazement. The cow lay panting on her side, looking wasted and forlorn.

"Is she okay?" Hannah asked, suddenly certain that such an Amazonian effort must have killed her.

"Shh," Ty said, and clasping her hand in his own, nodded toward the unfolding drama. "Watch."

She did, and finally, just when she was about to insist that they rush forward to help the pair, the calf raised its wobbly head and scrambled to get its legs under it. The cow sat up with a start, and bending her neck back, stared at the newborn with wide, startled eyes.

The calf struggled again. The cow bellowed, the sound low and throaty, a maternal call as old as time. Lurching to her feet, she hurried over to meet her newborn.

For some reason unknown to Hannah, tears stung her eyes as she watched the mother lick her baby dry. And when the calf finally rose, shaky and wet on its widespread legs, the first tear coursed down her cheek.

"You all right?" Ty's voice was low.

"Yes." Hannah wiped at the tear, feeling foolish. "Sorry. I'm not usually…" She wasn't usually what? Here—in a barn with a newborn calf and a man that made her feel a thousand things she should not be feeling now? "So silly."

One corner of his mouth lifted. "It's funny," he said, turning his attention to the heifer and her firstborn. "It's always miraculous. No matter how many times I see it."

"It doesn't seem like it would be a pretty thing to watch. And yet..." The mother lowed again and swiped her baby once more with her long, sandpaper tongue. "Now that I see it..."

"You've never seen a calf born before?"

His question caught her off guard. For a while she had forgotten that she'd been hired to care for stock. She was supposed to have some experience. But the truth was so obvious, and her reasons to keep it from him seemed so remote and ridiculous.

"Never," she said.

For a moment there was silence. Then, leaning forward, Tyrel pulled her into his arms and kissed her. In a moment he drew away.

"Thank you," he murmured.

"For what?"

"For the truth," he said, and kissed her again.

As a thousand sensations flamed through her, she shivered.

"We'd better go in. You're getting cold."

No, she wasn't. She was falling in love, drowning in desire, aching with need. But she said none of those things when he helped her to her feet.

Their journey to the house was slow and silent, but for the crunch of snow beneath their boots. With Tyrel's arm wrapped around her shoulders, Hannah felt as if she were floating along on nothing more substantial than a dream.

Inside the house, she removed her gloves and fumbled with her jacket zipper. She must be cold, she realized suddenly, for her fingers were ungainly. Taking them between his own hands, Ty blew his warm breath between his palms and rubbed her fingers gently.

Their eyes met. The kiss was inevitable, yielding, promising. But finally it came to an end. He unzipped her jacket himself. In a moment their outdoor clothing had been left behind and he was leading her into the kitchen where he urged her into a chair. Going to the refrigerator, he poured milk into a pan, warmed it, added a couple spoonfuls of powdered chocolate, and dumped it into cups.

"Here." Taking her hands again, he curled them around the mug. "It'll warm you up. Do you want marshmallows?"

"I've got to fit into my overalls," she reminded him.

"Oh, yeah," he said, and snorting, dropped two marshmallows into her brew. "If you were any skinnier we'd stick you on a pole in the garden."

"I'm afraid I feel more like the Wicked Witch than the Scarecrow lately," she said, and self-consciously tucked a whisper of hair behind her ear.

He watched the gesture and was stunned to think she might actually find herself lacking somehow. He pulled his gaze away with an effort and forced himself to sit down with his hot chocolate in front of him.

"So what about you, Hannah?" he asked softly. "Is there someone waiting for you somewhere?" His stomach roiled and his muscles felt tense as he said the words, but better to learn the truth now than later.

She stared into her mug. "I've got a father…somewhere."

Tyrel let the silence settle in for a moment. "I suppose it wouldn't be wise to admit I'm waiting on pins and needles for a real answer," he said.

"No." The word was nearly whispered. "There's no one waiting for me."

And there was a God in heaven.

"Why?" he murmured, unable to understand.

She scowled slightly as she swirled her chocolate, then cleared her throat. "Some men find me rather—cold."

His heart was making a strange hubbub in his chest. "I'm from North Dakota," he said. "What other people think is cold we find…" He stared at her as he tried to choose the proper words—*enchanting, intoxicating, mesmerizing.* "Damn near tropical," he said finally.

"Really?" she murmured, and for a moment he wondered if she had stopped breathing.

"Yeah," he said, and kissed her again.

The next three hours passed like so many seconds. They talked of everything from movies to horseshoes, skydiving to powdered milk, until finally Ty urged her to her feet and toward the stairs.

"You'd better go to bed," he said, and though he knew he was a cad, he couldn't help adding, "Alone?"

She nodded, but the motion was slow and less than enthusiastic.

There was not only a God, but He was kind.

Smiling, Ty escorted Hannah to her room, and there in the doorway, he kissed her good-night.

"Sorry I kept you up so late," he murmured, knowing it was a lie, that he wouldn't trade a moment of the time they had spent together. "Sleep in late tomorrow. It's Sunday."

"And the cows don't need to be fed on Sunday?"

"Not by you," he said, and because he couldn't stop himself, he kissed her again, then drew a heavy breath, trying to tear himself away. It didn't work. "You're sure you won't be lonely in there all by yourself?"

"I've got Sean," she whispered.

"Those movie stars have all the luck." One more kiss. Just one more. But it stretched out. "Maybe I should check under your bed. For bogeymen?" he said, letting his kisses slip to her throat.

She leaned back against the doorjamb, breathing hard, her eyes closed and her slim fingers clasped in his shirt.

He kissed the tiny hollow between her collarbone, then moved lower, breathing in her scent, her presence, the very essence of her.

"Ty, please…" Her hands tightened, pushing him away. The kiss ended. Her eyes opened, finding his. "I'm not ready."

Tyrel stared into her eyes, then, clamping a tight hand on his more feral urges, he managed one step back. "Sorry."

"Don't be," she whispered, and reaching out, laid a soft palm against his cheek.

He blew out a breath and tried to relax.

"Are you okay?" she asked.

"Me? Hell, yeah."

She smiled a little.

"I'll just…" He nodded toward the stairs. "I'll just go have myself a roll in the snow. I'll be fine."

She laughed, the sound low and seductive. "*I'm* sorry."

"No." Leaning forward, he kissed her lightly on the cheek. "Good night, Hannah. Sleep in," he repeated, and managed, to his utter amazement, to walk away.

DESPITE HER BEST EFFORTS to sleep in as Ty had suggested, Hannah awoke just after seven. She'd had four hours of sleep, and yet she felt as if she could fly.

Sitting up, she glanced out her window. The sun shone out of a robin's egg sky. Feeling giddy, she hugged her legs for a moment before hopping out of bed.

Beneath the weak shower spray, she sang a few lines from a Garth Brooks song, then laughed at her feeble attempt. Glancing in the mirror, she decided rouge was unnecessary, and foundation somehow seemed silly here. So she swiped her lashes with a little mascara, and still humming, pulled on a fresh pair of jeans and a button-down shirt, then hustled downstairs.

The kitchen was deserted. Impatient to see Tyrel, she slipped into her borrowed jacket, then stopped herself at the door. What was wrong with her? She was a Vandegard and a Clifton. She couldn't pursue a man.

Of course not, she thought. She'd go feed Daniel and run into Ty by *accident*.

Giggling, she mixed the calf replacer into a bucket of warm water and hurried out the door.

"SO, BROTHER, LOOKS LIKE I owe you some money, huh?" Nate said.

He'd returned home just before dawn and must be tired as

hell. But he looked as bright eyed and irritating as usual, Ty thought.

"What are you talking about?" he asked, pushing a white-faced calf into a stall as Nate shooed the worried cow in after.

"Your expression," Nate said, pulling the gate shut only enough so that Ty could hurry back out before the new mother took offense at his presence.

He did so now. They pulled the gate firmly closed and glanced over the top two-by-four at the pair. They would be fine, just needed a little solitary confinement to help them bond properly.

"What about my expression?" Ty asked, scowling at his younger brother.

Nate grinned square back into his face. "Yep. While the cats were away, the mice were aplay."

"You're nuts," Ty said, and turning, fetched a half bale of straw and tossed it into the newly occupied stall. Taking a pitchfork from the wall, he stepped inside and spread the bedding.

"Nuts, am I?" Nate asked, watching his brother work. "Maybe so, but if there's one thing I know, it's love in the country." Putting his hand dramatically over his heart, he burst into his usual inane lyrics.

Finished with his job, Ty stepped from the stall and closed the gate behind him. "The wonderful thing about you, Nate, is you can talk forever about nothing."

"'Cuz," Nate continued, ignoring his brother's words as he followed him toward the door, "the bet was *she* had to kiss *you*. And not the other way around. There's a fine distinction there."

Ty hung the fork near the door and turned away.

"So which was it?" Nate continued, dogging him like a heeler on a recalcitrant bull. "Did she kiss you or not? 'Cuz I'm sure not gonna fork over that ten bucks unless she took the initiative."

Ty stopped near the door, remembering Hannah in the barn, in his arms, in his dreams. He couldn't forget the euphoric feelings of the night before, but they were now mingled with an inexplicable foreboding and a nagging fear. He and Hannah came from different worlds. Although he knew almost nothing about her, he knew that much, and his ravaging desire for her would not change that. "I think I might be in over my head, Nate," he murmured.

"Yeah?" Nate's grin only broadened. "She *did* kiss you!" he crowed. "So she ain't the ice princess you thought she was, huh?"

Disgusted and confused, Ty pushed open the door. "Shut up, N—" he began, but before he finished the words, a bucket of milk hit him square in the face.

He gasped and stumbled back, arms spread wide. "Hannah!"

She stood before him, eyes blazing.

"A bet?" she said, her voice low.

"Hannah…" He felt breathless and stupid. "It's not like it sounds."

"Not like it sounds?" Her voice was shrill. "Then you didn't make a bet about me?"

Ty winced. "I didn't know you then."

"You don't know me now!" she snapped.

He reached out to touch her arm. She smacked his hand away.

"How much would you have won if I'd have *slept* with you?" she asked.

"Dammit, Hannah, it's not like that!" Ty said, grabbing her arm again.

She swung the plastic bucket like a spiked mace, then threw it ferociously to the ground and stomped off.

He lunged after her, but Nate snagged his jacket, holding him back.

"Listen, Tyrel," he said, voice low as he watched Hannah run for the house. "Sometimes you're dense as a rock, but you're my only brother and I don't want to see you killed." He nodded toward Hannah's fleeing figure. "You'd better wait till she cools down."

Ty loosened his fists and blew out a hard breath. The milk was starting to congeal on his face and had seeped down his chest and into his underwear. "How long do you think that will be?"

"Oh…" Nate shook his head once. "Remember Grandpa Ben. He was still spry well into his nineties. There's hope you'll live so long."

THE DAYS PASSED with painful slowness. Twice Ty tried to speak to Hannah, but both times she managed to evade the issue. On the second attempt, he'd nearly lost his fingers in the door she slammed.

But he could wait no longer. Today they would have this out if he had to wrestle her down and sit on her. He hoped it wouldn't come to that because he was too young to die.

"I've got to talk to you," he said.

She didn't stop bedding the calf pen. In fact, she didn't turn to look at him when she spoke. "Of course, Mr. Fox. You're the boss."

"Hannah." He stared in frustration at her profile. She'd discarded the tweed cap he'd loaned her. Her hair, bright as summer wheat, swung gently as she continued to spread a soft, golden layer of straw for her small charges. "I owe you an apology. I shouldn't have made that stupid bet." She continued working, her movements graceful, her expression unchanged. "But I didn't know you then. I thought you were just a spoiled little rich girl who thought herself too good for the likes of me. I thought you wouldn't last a day. But here you are, working…" He paused, searching for words as he watched her. She had hung her jacket on a nail, and now wore faded jeans and one of his cast-off shirts. The wearsoftened flannel caressed her shoulders and breasts, making her look small and so feminine it was all he could do to not pull her into his arms and beg for her forgiveness. "Working like a storm trooper," he murmured. "With your hair all soft and your…" He blew out another breath, his mouth dry. "It's no secret that you're beautiful, Hannah. Not to you. Not to anyone. And I was all tied up in knots. With you so haughty, and me looking like a country hick. And I made that idiotic bet. But that wasn't why I kissed you. I was just overwh—''

"So we have a new calf?" she interrupted, still not looking at him.

Tyrel tightened his jaw. "Are you listening to me?"

She straightened and stared at him in mock surprise. "Why, no, Mr. Fox, I'm not. I said you could talk. I didn't say I would listen."

"Dammit it, Hannah, I—"

"He's lonely."

"What?"

"The new calf. What happened to his mother?"

Ty ran splayed fingers through his hair and contemplated pulling it out. "She can't get up. It happens sometimes after a hard labor. Maybe in a day or two she'll be on her feet. Listen, I—"

"He'll need colostrum. And we're out."

"Dammit, will you—"

"You'll have to get some for him. Or I can collect it myself if you tell me where to go."

She faced him squarely, as if challenging him to do just that.

Tension steamed between them.

"I think I've fallen in love with you, Hannah," he said softly, laying all his cards on the table, taking that awful risk that could well break him.

She stared at him for a moment, her expression open, her eyes vulnerable. He dared not breathe. Then suddenly her expression became closed, and her eyes went hard. She laughed out loud, and the sound was harsh and cold.

"In love with me? And you think I care? Or that I should be surprised. You're hardly the first man to tell me that. You're simply the boldest. What a nerve you have! You think I'd ever become serious about you—" Her voice broke, and for an instant, he wondered if she was about to cry. But it was a foolish thought. "A two-bit North Dakota cowboy on a broken-down ranch. Do you know who I am? Do you have any idea?''

Tyrel tightened his jaw. Anger flooded in, ripping through him like a January wind. ''I don't give a damn who you are.''

For a moment her face went pale and something showed in her eyes. Sadness? Loneliness? Hope? But it was gone in a second, drowned beneath her pummeled pride.

''I'm here until you pay me and no longer,'' she said, her voice low. ''Six more days and I'm out of this nightmare.''

They stared at each other, then Ty turned away and left the barn.

''SO YOU'RE WORKING for the Fox boys.'' Ed Norton was a small, narrow man with a two-day beard and eyes that resembled the placid Holsteins' he milked with his son-in-law and two daughters.

''Yes, I am,'' Hannah said. Having no wish to talk to Ty again, she'd asked Nate for directions and come for the colostrum herself.

''They must be having some trouble with their herd, huh? Lose some mommas, did they?'' he asked, glancing stiffly over his shoulder as he puttered into the milking parlor. Six cows stood in a row on a concrete slab four feet above the floor. Their heads were in stanchions. They munched contentedly while octopuslike machines slurped at their udders.

''Some,'' she said, staring at the strange apparatus. Her mood was as black as sin. All she wanted was to collect the colostrum and leave.

''Yeah, them babies gotta have that colostrum. Gives 'em their first antibodies, ya know. And our cows give so danged much milk, we don't need all that rich stuff. Best herd in the state,'' he said, then nodded at his own words. But his thick brows were beetled over his watery eyes now. ''Best herd in the state, and that's 'cuz we know how to cull,'' he murmured, reaching up to pat a bony Holstein on the shoulder. ''I gotta do it, Betty. Gotta do it.''

She just wanted to leave, Hannah reminded herself. Leave

the milking barn, the state, maybe even the country. But she was staring at the old man now, and was almost certain his chin was quivering.

"What do you have to do?" she asked.

"I gotta sell her." His voice broke.

"Sell her?" Hannah straightened her back. The nearest cow turned from her grain, still chewing, and suddenly the image of Bette Davis flashed through Hannah's mind. The bovine eyes were just like the woman's. "You mean for slaughter?"

"She's been with me nigh unto ten years," he said. "My wife, God rest her soul, named her. But she don't hardly give eight gallons anymore."

"Eight gallons! A day?"

"Barely half what she used to do. Still…I…" He shook his head and patted her again. "She's been a good old girl. See them kind eyes."

She did. "Mr. Norton," she said, pursing her lips and coming to a quick decision. "I'd like to make you a proposition."

Half an hour later, Hannah was back at The Lone Oak. Behind her, Ed Norton drove up pulling a stock trailer.

Stepping out of the Jimmy, Hannah didn't deign to glance at Tyrel, though she saw him coming out of the barn. He crossed the muddy yard with long, quick strides.

Ed creaked from behind the wheel of his old Dodge. "Tyrel," he said by way of greeting.

"Ed." Ty nodded and reached out to shake the old man's hand, his arm half-bare where he'd rolled back the sleeve of his denim shirt. "What brings you out this way?"

"It's the girl here." Ed chuckled, and nodded toward Hannah who stood nearby.

"The girl?" Ty moved toward her. There was suspicion in his eyes and a thousand other emotions she refused to try to decipher. Instead, she met his gaze evenly.

"You're purchasing Mr. Norton's cow," she said.

"Purchasing—"

"I'll be putting her in with the bottle calves," she informed him.

For a moment his expression registered nothing but shock. Then he gritted a smile at her. "Over my dead body."

"Why, Mr. Fox...." She smiled back. Tension snapped between them. "You're giving me goose bumps."

Ed cleared his throat. "Yeah," he said, bobbing his head and glancing nervously from one intense face to the other. "She's a heck of a nice cow. And a good mother. She don't cut it as a milker no more, but she could nurse a bundle of calves. It's a damn fine idea. Wish I'd a thought of it myself. The son-in-law though, he'd bust a gasket if I tried a stunt like this—always wanting to modernize, modernize. But Betty..." He pursed his lips as if holding back tears. "She'll do the job for ya."

"Ed," Tyrel said, "if you'll excuse us for a moment..." Taking Hannah's arm, he pulled her off to the side.

"Listen, honey," he said. "You might think you're God's gift to mankind, but you're not going to come sashaying in here and take over my ranch."

"You listen, cowboy," she said, jabbing a finger at his chest. "So far you've got three calves without mothers. Before you're done that number will probably double. As it is I spend half my day feeding babies. Betty was made for the job."

"What the hell do you think you're doing here?" he asked, his voice low.

"I think I'm getting a mother for your calves."

"Well, you're not," he said. "You're screwing with my ranch. And when you screw with my ranch, you screw with me."

"Believe me, Mr. Fox, that's the furthest thing from my intentions," she snapped.

He glared at her. "This animal isn't going to let those calves nurse," he said, waving toward the trailer. "If you knew anything about cattle, you'd know that."

"Ed said she would."

"Well, Ed's a sentimental old fool who blubbers at every auction. She's a milk cow not a foster mother."

Hannah raised her brows and glared up at him like a princess with a peasant. "She'll do the job I got her to do."

She'd said something very similar about Pansy. It pained Ty no end to think she might be right again, and he wasn't going down without a fight. "Oh? And does your vast experience tell you that, Ms. Nelson?"

"That's right," she said.

"Geez! They're bottle calves, Hannah, not Romanian orphans."

"They're living beings," she growled, yanking her arm from his grasp. "With hearts and minds and feelings. Or have you forgotten about feelings, Mr. Fox?"

Their gazes fused and snapped.

"Bring her out," Ty ordered, turning on his heel and striding toward the trailer. "I'll put her in the barn."

"So ol' Betty's working out pretty good, huh?" Nate asked, glancing over his milk glass at Hannah.

"Yes."

"That was a fine idea you had," Nate said, then nodded toward his brother. "Wasn't it a fine idea, brother?"

Ty snorted into his coffee.

It had been six days since he'd kissed her, six days since he'd handed her his heart. Six days since she'd sliced it into ribbons. He hated her for that. And she'd be leaving in ninety-four hours. Good riddance to her!

But greenhorn that she was, she'd made a difference in this ranch. She'd slaved over Daniel, convinced him to eat. Saved his life, really. And the other orphans—they were growing in leaps and bounds, not stunted and scraggly like bottle calves often were, but actually gaining more weight than some of the calves who were with their real moms.

She'd hired Pansy to cook and clean, freeing them up to fully concentrate on the ranch work. And she'd started ground work on the young horses. He'd watched her. Ty had been meaning to halterbreak the yearlings himself. Hell, he'd been meaning to halterbreak the two-year-olds. It was a crime really, that he was so far behind on his horse work. They'd be a lot harder to train now that they were older.

But Hannah had a way about her. You wouldn't know it to look at her cool exterior, but she could reach a horse like few others could. Ty glanced across the table at her. His heart pitched. Not that he cared about her. Hell, he may be a masochist, and he may be an idiot, but he wasn't a masochistic idiot.

He didn't know why she was here, but he knew she wouldn't be for long. And good riddance, like he'd already said.

But she did have good hands. He remembered watching her as she'd calmed Platinum's yearling. She was a tall, dappled gray filly with endless legs and big spooky eyes. But by the time Hannah was through with her, she'd stood like an old cart horse, half asleep as Hannah ran her hands over her dappled coat.

How would it feel to have her touch him like that? To feel her fingers feather soft against his skin.

Geez! Ty jerked himself abruptly to his feet.

"Where you going?" Pansy barked from the stove.

"Going to bed," Ty said.

"You ain't hardly ate nothing." She said it like an accusation.

"I've had enough," he said, and he had, enough of thinking of Hannah, dreaming of Hannah, watching Hannah. Enough and not nearly enough.

"Go ahead then," Pansy said, miffed. She did her duties with militant seriousness and to her own way of thinking, her duty was to add fifty pounds to each of their weights. "Hannah," she said, turning from Ty as if he were a traitor not worthy of her concern. "You got a letter today."

"A letter?" Hannah glanced up.

Ty turned in the doorway and watched her. Her gaze flickered to him and away. His stomach turned over. Who was the letter from? What was it about?

He didn't know and didn't care, he reminded himself, and repeated it a hundred times before sleep finally took him.

NERVOUS AND UNCERTAIN, Hannah sat on her bed and opened the letter.

Her father's scrawled handwriting winked up at her. She took a deep breath and read.

"My dearest Hannah." She frowned at the use of her assumed name.

> I hope all is well with you.
>
> As for me, I am fine. I miss our home. Or perhaps just the opportunity to return there. Strange how we don't realize what we've got until we can no longer have it.
>
> Which brings me to my reason for writing. Perhaps it's my advancing age that makes me realize what a hopeless parent I have been. But I realize it now, and I wish with all my heart that I could redo those years.
>
> All the life I have lived, all the melodrama I have witnessed, one would think I would have seen what was most important.
>
> You. Your happiness. And it is you I have failed with my endless days away from you. My endless obsession with my own success.
>
> Please forgive me. I hope you have found something I neglected to give you. Real life. Not just the cheap fiction that has filled my days. But something lasting and true.
>
> I wish I could see you now. I wish I could make up for those years, but I cannot.
>
> Please, Hannah, no matter what you do, do *not* return home, or indeed, to any of the haunts where you might be recognized. Don't try to contact me. Any call might

be traced. Stay where you are. You are safe there. And I would surely die if you were lost to me now.

All my love,
Daddy

Hannah let the letter droop in her fingers. What did he mean, he had failed her? It wasn't true. He had been a good father. It was she who was the failure. He had given her everything, every trinket, every garment, every vehicle she had asked for. True, sometimes it had taken tears, and sometimes it had taken tantrums, but eventually she'd always gotten her way, until this last disagreement.

No matter what she did, she'd been unable to change his mind about her leaving LA, about coming here. *You must leave before it's too late,* he'd said. And now he spoke of the things she had missed. But what things? She'd had everything from tennis instructions to daily room service. And yet…

She shifted on the bed, then stretched her arms above her head. Suddenly the image of a dark man with musical laughter and entrancing eyes came to mind for the zillionth time. A man who had touched her and kissed her and made her heart…

Springing from the bed, Hannah began to pace.

Tyrel Fox meant nothing to her. Indeed, he was far beneath her. And he had laughed at her, bet that he could bring the ice princess to her knees. And all the time she had been falling in love.…

No! Foolishness.

Reaching the window, she gazed out onto the rolling pastures beyond the yard. The snow had melted, leaving only tired, spotty patches of dirty white.

She hated Tyrel Fox, she told herself. But regardless of her feelings, it looked as if she would be staying awhile longer.

8

HANNAH PULLED the buckskin to a halt. He was a two-year-old with a two-year-old's energy, and a two-year-old's attention span. Peppy's Dillon Dude was the name on his registration papers. She rubbed his forehead, wondering if he'd been named after Matt Dillon's buckskin. He looked much the same as that movie horse, only better, longer legs, finer neck.

Tyrel Fox may be an immature, dishonest, mean-spirited, half-witted, down-on-his-luck... Well, in short he was a jerk, but he *did* know his horses.

Hannah let her attention stray over the fence. Several of the young animals were lying flat out on their sides, exposing as much area of their bodies to the sun as possible. Nate's palomino mare stood with one hip cocked and her lower lip drooping. All the horses looked drugged by the sunshine. All except Maverick. He reared on his hind legs again, trying to coax a yearling to play with him.

He would look good under an English saddle. With those legs and that drive, he'd jump like a deer. Not that the Tyrant would ever allow his cowboy horse to be used that way, but...

Hannah stroked the buckskin's neck as she thought.

She hadn't told Ty about the letter she'd received from her father, of course. Neither had she broached the subject of her staying on. It was entirely possible he wouldn't allow it. But what else could she do? Daddy had begged her to remain where she was, and because of that she had no choice. But her pride wouldn't let her admit her predicament to a barbarian like Tyrel Fox.

No. She wouldn't sacrifice her pride. But maybe...

"MR. FOX."

Tyrel sent his lariat loop flying over a plastic steer's head that had been stuck into a hay bale. Snapping up the slack, he turned to her, his eyes flat, his expression inscrutable.

She held his gaze and raised her chin a fraction of an inch. "I need to speak to you."

"Yeah?" he said, staring at her for a moment before striding off to retrieve his loop from the dummy steer.

She clasped her hands together, knowing she'd be a fool to show her emotions.

"I have a proposition for you," she said, forcing her arms back to her sides and hoping the posture looked more natural than it felt.

"Do you now?" He coiled up his rope.

"Yes." She refused to clear her throat. "I've decided to stay on awhile longer—but only if I can train Maverick to jump."

He was still for a moment, then laughed.

She wasn't going to get mad, she told herself. She couldn't afford to get mad. "May I ask what you find so amusing?" she asked finally.

"You," he said. Having apparently gained control of his humor, he flipped and caught his loop with practiced ease. "You are, honey."

"God knows, it's my sole goal in life to entertain you," she said.

"Well, you sure as hell do." He tossed the loop again. It settled easily over the dummy.

"Do you have an English saddle?" she asked. She'd learned with Daddy that it was best to treat her wishes as though it was a foregone conclusion that they would be met.

"English saddle?" He chuckled again. "No. I sure don't."

"Then you'll have to buy one," she said, her tone stiff.

He chuckled. "So you can teach Maverick to jump?"

"That's right."

"There's just one problem," he said, retrieving his loop again. "I don't want Maverick to jump. He's a roping horse."

His expression was smug, his attitude irritating—but she wasn't going to get mad.

"He's not a roping horse," she said, and managed a gritty smile.

"That just goes to show that you don't know any more about horses than you do about anything else."

Anger rolled over her like a high tide. "Listen, you goon," she snarled. "He's no more a roping horse than I am a cocktail waitress."

"Well, honey," he said, staring at her, "you dress yourself in one of them short skirts and get that big-hair thing going, that just might be an option."

She caught her breath. Did that mean he wouldn't let her stay? But she couldn't allow herself to think that way. "He's built like a Thoroughbred," she argued, refusing to take his bait, to be sidetracked. "He's born to jump. A natural."

"What do you know about natural?" he asked. "Natural means honest. And, honey, that's something you don't know the first thing about."

"Why? Because any *natural* woman would fall for your two-bit charm? Because any *natural* woman would be entranced by the sight of your eyes, would die for the strength of your arms around her, would be struck speechless at the sound of…" Her words trailed off, and for the life of her, she couldn't remember how she'd gotten started on this track.

He was staring at her, his sensual lips slightly parted, his brows raised over his mahogany eyes.

She blinked twice and considered hiding behind the roping dummy like a whipped cur. But a Clifton Vandegard didn't hide. "Maverick's a…a natural," she finished lamely, finding her line of thought with some difficulty.

He exhaled a soft breath finally, staring at her as if trying to read something in her expression. "And where did you get your horse knowledge, Hannah? Kentucky?"

"That's none of your business."

A muscle jumped in his jaw. His brows lowered. "I think I have a right to know a few things about my employees—such as…oh, I don't know—why the hell they're here!" he said, leaning into her face.

She tried to hold his gaze, but finally looked away. "Listen," she said, glancing at the horses in the pasture. "You want to build a reputation for your stallion. But you're not going to do it. Not unless you get some of his babies out there winning ribbons."

"His babies'll win," he said. "Belt buckles—for roping!" He took a few strides toward her.

"I can make that horse jump. I can make him fly."

"I don't want him to jump. I don't want him to fly. In fact, I don't want any of your prissy city ways or your prissy city tack or—"

"Prissy!" She crunched her fists tight and gritted her teeth. "I am not prissy! I've worked off my…" She could think of a thousand appropriate things to say, but her mother's words were still perfectly clear in her mind. *A lady does not use profanity.*

"Your what?" he asked.

"I've worked my…fingers off for you! And—"

His laughter interrupted her. "And you have such pretty little…*fingers,*" he said. "But the fact remains, I'm not going to let you spoil that horse."

"Spoil him!" She spat the words.

"An animal like that needs a firm hand, not some soft—"

"I am not soft!"

He grinned as he let his gaze sweep down her body, as if thinking of parts of her anatomy that were just that.

She gritted her teeth. "I can do anything you Barbarian Brothers can do!"

"Yeah?" He raised his brows at her. "The Barbarian Brothers can team rope. Can you do that?"

"A retarded chimpanzee could do that. And probably with more panache."

He canted his head at her. "More what?"

She snorted at his ignorance.

He growled back at her. "So you're saying you can rope."

"Of course I can!"

"Then come on." He raised the lariat toward her.

She blinked. Her temper settled a notch. "Well, I didn't say…" She paused and swallowed. She couldn't lose this job. "I didn't say right now. I'd need a little time."

"Oh." He laughed. "How much time are we talking about, Ms. Nelson?"

She had no idea. "Three weeks?" They were the first words that came to mind.

"So you're saying you could rope a steer in three weeks?"

He was laughing at her. Maybe a lady didn't swear, but her mother hadn't said anything about not knocking a man on his sexy ass.

"Your steer doesn't look like it's going to run all that fast," she said, nodding toward the dummy head.

"Oh, no," he said, shaking out his loop. "Not *that* steer. A *real* steer with legs and ears and horns. You know. The breathing kind?"

"Real steer?"

"Uh-huh. From a real horse. That's how we do it up here on my broken-down, two-bit ranch."

She shouldn't have insulted his ranch. He was so touchy about that.

"You're not…" He took a few steps closer, eyeing her as if she were a strange new breed. "You're not scared, are you? You're not thinking there might be something you can't do."

She tightened her jaw. "Three weeks will be fine. And after that time I start Maverick English."

"Wait a minute," he said. "What do I get out of this? The privilege of your company?"

"What do you want?" she asked, her tone cautious.

He laughed again. "Now there's a hell of a question for a

lady like you to be asking.'' He walked around her, studying her as if judging her for soundness. ''Aren't you afraid I might ask for something *revolting?* To touch you or… Geez! What if I wanted to *kiss* you or something.''

The memory of his kiss sent a spurt of warmth up from her belly. ''What do you want?'' she asked again, holding his gaze and making certain her tone was icy cold.

He stood there in silence for a moment, head tilted sideways as he watched her, and then he said, ''I want you to sing to me.''

''What?''

He nodded, as if it were the perfect solution. ''Yeah. I want you to sing me a love song. At the rodeo.''

''Wh—''

''Yeah. Let's see. Three weeks from now…'' He narrowed his eyes in thought. ''That'll be about the time of the Buffalo rodeo. And they got a hell of a sound system there.''

''Sound system!''

''Yeah. I can hear it now. Course you'll need to tell everyone you're singing it for me.''

''I don't…'' She backed off a step. ''I don't sing really well.''

He nodded. ''You're sure as hell right about that, honey. I heard you in the shower. You couldn't carry a tune if it were tattooed on your ass.''

She huffed.

''But—'' he shrugged ''—if losing scares you—''

''I will not lose!''

He grinned. ''It's a deal then?'' he asked, sticking out his hand.

She grasped his hand in roiling terror.

He stepped back. ''I gotta put up with you for three more weeks then,'' he said.

''Yes.'' She gritted her teeth. ''Three more long weeks,'' she agreed, but in her mind she breathed a heavy sigh. At least she was here for a while longer.

Dropping her hand, Ty turned quickly away, before she

could see his expression, before she could sense his relief. He'd just won himself three more weeks, and if there was a God in heaven—maybe longer.

"Good morning, Nathan," Hannah said, bending over slightly to speak to the booted feet that stuck out from under a tractor.

She'd checked the bottle calves and fed the horses, and then, when she was certain Tyrel was occupied elsewhere, she had hurried over to the machine shed where she'd seen Nathan disappear.

He slid out from under a John Deere tractor and grinned at her. A streak of grease was smeared across his right cheek. "Hey," he said. "How're you doing?"

"Good." She nodded. "How about you?"

"Good."

"That's nice." She cleared her throat. "So you have a band?"

"Yeah. The Restless Cowboys."

She drew a deep breath and remembered not to wring her hands.

"Were you needing something, Hannah?"

"No." She said the word too quickly and silently berated herself. Of course she needed something. She needed a lobotomy for making such an idiotic bet. But short of that, she needed help and lots of it.

"Well, then…" Nathan grinned at her, contracting the grease stain on his cheek. "I better get to it," he said, pulling his creeper back under the tractor.

"Nathan," she said. Her voice sounded panicked to her own ears.

He pushed himself back out. His grin had expanded, though she wouldn't have thought it possible. "The way I see it, we got us two options," he said. "We can either teach you to sing, or we can teach you to rope. But I heard your singing…" he said, and shook his head.

The air left her lungs in a rush. "You know about the bet?"

"Heard it through the grapevine. So I figure..." He slid back under. She watched him disappear and reappear a second later.

He sat up, and there, clasped in his right hand, was a lariat. She felt her jaw drop.

"I'm your man," he said.

Moments later they stood near the roping dummy.

"So which you want to do, headin' or heelin'?" he asked.

"Huh?"

He grinned, nonplussed. "Ever tossed a rope before?"

"No."

"Ever handled a rope before?"

"No."

"Ever seen a rope before?"

"It's that thing you have in your hand, right?"

"All right. Battle's half won. Now you gotta rope a steer, right?"

"Right."

"Well, then—"

"Nathan?"

"Yeah?"

"What's a steer?"

He paled a little. "Tell me you're joking and I'll continue this lesson."

"And if I don't?"

"I might cry. 'Cuz it really tears me up inside to see Ty win a bet."

"Okay, well in that case, I was joking."

"Good," he said, making no attempt to make her think he believed her. "Now listen, Hannah, there's a couple different types of roping. But what me and Ty do is called team roping."

"Which involves a steer," she said.

"That's right." He winced. "A steer. Now some of them steers have horns and some don't. But all of them got spunk, and none of them much care for the idea of getting trussed up like Penelope Pitstop on the train track. You see, we put them in a chute about here.'' Bending down, he picked up a stick and drew an *X* in the mud. "Then we put a horse and rider on his right side and a horse and rider on his left side." He drew corresponding marks. "The steer is released. The first cowboy takes off after him and tosses a loop around his head. The second cowboy runs around the steer..." Nate curved a line around the steer's mark. "...and ropes his heels."

"His heels?"

"Yeah. His hind legs."

"You're kidding," she said, certain he was.

But he wasn't. "Nope. So which would you like to do?"

She blinked. "Which is easier?"

"The headin'."

"Then that's what I want to do."

"Good idea. Okay." Retrieving his rope from the ground, he rose and began twirling his loop. It grew larger with no visible exertion on his part. "Now, one of the first things to understand is, you don't rope a steer from the front. Unless the steer is brain-dead, he ain't gonna just stand there and wait for you to come get him. So you'll be approaching him from behind like this."

Twirling his loop over his head now, he took a few strides toward the dummy, and then, with practiced ease, he let the loop fly. It soared as easy and sure as a sparrow in flight and fell with fluid grace over the dummy's wide horns.

"You see?" He turned back toward her. "Nothing to it."

"Right."

"Okay. You try it," he said, and handed her the rope.

She took it gingerly.

"It ain't going to bite you."

"I know," she said, trying to figure out what to do with thirty feet of stiff nylon that had a bad attitude and a mind of its own.

"Here." He stepped up behind her, settled his left hand on her left and his right on her right. "You gotta hold it just so. Then when it feels right just swing it a little."

He guided her hands, twirling the loop gently beside them. "Loosen up. Take the rhythm of the rope," he said, moving slightly closer behind her. "Yeah, that..." He cleared his throat. He was standing close enough for her to feel the muscles flex in his chest, but she was concentrating hard on the task at hand. "That feels good. And it looks good, too. Don't that look good, Ty?"

Hannah jumped and spun about, dropping the rope. Ty stood not twenty feet away, glaring at her. Nate chuckled, and though Hannah called herself a thousand kinds of fool, she felt herself blush. Turning, Ty strode off toward the barn.

"He's always been the jealous type. Okay, let's try that again," Nate said, handing her the rope. "Swing it by your side a little."

She did so, but she was distracted now and the loop kept slipping away, while the remainder of the rope had a tendency to snake off in sloppy folds down her left leg.

"That's good. That's not bad," Nate lied. "Now bring it up above your head."

She did. It hit her left ear and settled over her shoulders at a stubborn angle.

"Okay, well..." Nate said, rocking back on one heel and sheepishly scratching his nose. "I think you might want to cancel any late-night plans you got going for about the next, uh...three weeks or so."

LATE NIGHT PLANS! Hannah flopped into bed like a beached fish, then wished she hadn't because the ripple effect of the mattress made her arms bounce, and her arms shouldn't be bouncing. Her arms shouldn't be moving at all. She wasn't even sure they should still be attached to her body.

Turning her head, she groaned into the coverlet.

"Hey, Hannah." The door creaked open behind her. "You looked pretty good out there," Ty said. The door closed.

Hannah squeezed her eyes shut and wished for death. Either his or hers—she couldn't decide which, but in a moment the door opened again and he was still breathing.

"Tomorrow, though," Ty said, "you might want to try roping the dummy instead of your shoulders."

BY 6:30 THE NEXT MORNING Hannah's skin was lobster red from the beating of the hot shower. By seven she could almost move her arms. By nine she had fed the horses, cleaned the stalls and dragged the roping dummy inside the barn.

She wasn't about to give up, but she'd be hanged by her thumbs until she was dead before she would entertain Tyrel Fox with her roping antics again.

By ten o'clock she thought she might die. By noon, she hoped she would.

It took every ounce of her energy to keep from falling face first into her potatoes again.

"Tired?" Ty asked, watching her over his coffee cup.

"No!" She straightened with a start.

He grinned like a devil, like a satyr, like a lover. "Good. 'Cuz I need you to go to town for me. We got some calves with scours. You'll have to pick up some Baytril from Doc Haberman."

"No problem."

He snorted, then rose to his feet. "That's nice to hear 'cuz I'm all burned out, and I'm going to need you to take a couple of shifts during the night."

"All right."

"All right," he said, and pivoting on his heel, left the house.

Nate chuckled and helped himself to another helping of scalloped potatoes. "Geez, I love seeing him like this."

Hannah knew she shouldn't ask, but she couldn't help herself. "Like what?"

Nate turned to her and grinned. "All tied up in knots," he said, and dug into his third serving.

SHE WAS THE ONE all tied up in knots, Hannah thought. *Literally.* Several days had passed, but still the muscles in her shoulders were knotted like a bowline. Her back ached as if someone had been flogging her with a frayed rope. And her arms... Well, her arms weren't even worth thinking about.

And she stunk!

Ben-Gay. If someone had told her four months ago that Allissa Clifton Vandegard would someday be roping a plastic steer and smearing her body with Ben-Gay, she would have laughed in his face. But now she was too sore to laugh. And Ben-Gay had been the only relief she could find in the drugstore in Valley Green.

Groaning out loud, she slipped out of bed.

According to the clock beside her bed it was one o'clock in the morning—time for her to check the cattle.

Five minutes later she was dressed and heading out the door.

From his bedroom window, Tyrel watched her make her way across the yard toward the pastures.

She was a big girl, he reminded himself—all grown-up. Hell, she was meaner than any animal out there, and could damn well take care of herself.

Still... He paced again. What if something happened to her? Striding back to the window, he stared out into the night. Half-frozen raindrops were pinging against the windowpane. He should have gone out himself.

The hell he should have! He was paying her and paying her well! She could damn well do her part.

Staring through the darkness, he watched her climb through the fence, watched her bend so that her fanny and her endless legs were all he could see.

He was out the door in thirty-two seconds. But there he stopped. What was he going to tell her? That he was worried about her? That he couldn't sleep knowing she was out there alone? Hell, why didn't he just tell her he was in love with her, couldn't breathe when she was near him, couldn't think when she was in the same...universe?

A bull bellowed, and the sound gave Ty an idea. Stepping back inside, he unhooked a cane from the wall and stashed it beneath his arm. If Hannah saw him slinking around after her, and he hoped she wouldn't, he'd say he'd thought Houdini had gotten out again, and he'd come armed to chase him back in.

In a few moments, Ty could see Hannah, barely illuminated by the barnyard light as she moved between the clusters of cattle ahead of him. He stood on the lee side of a huge, round bale, sheltered both from the rain and her view.

Geez, he was an idiot, he thought. Hooking the cane on his arm, he shoved his bare hands into the pockets of his jacket and gave her time to finish her tour of the pasture.

This kind of cold was worse than the dead of winter. He pulled up his collar and called himself ten kinds of a fool. He could be fast asleep in his nice warm bed about now. Shaking his head at his own lunacy, he turned toward the house.

Then her shriek brought him up cold.

9

TY STREAKED DOWN THE HILL. "Hannah!" he yelled.

He found her on the ground, her pale face turned up. Not ten yards away stood a black cow with steam billowing from its nostrils.

"Hannah! Stay down."

But she was already rising to her feet, and the cow, incensed, dove at her again.

There was nothing Ty could do but fling himself between them and swing the cane with all his might. It smacked across the cow's tender nose and splintered in two.

Bellowing in surprise, the Angus skittered to a halt, shook her head once, then turned tail and ran.

Ty rushed to Hannah, breathing her name as he bent down beside her. "Are you all right?"

"Cranky II?" she asked, her voice barely audible over her hiss of pain.

"What?"

"That must have been your token mean cow," she said, trying to rise.

"Stay there," he ordered, pressing her back down.

She did so with a groan.

"Where do you hurt?" His heart was slowing a little, and he could almost breathe again.

She winced. "You don't want to know where I hurt."

"Where did she hit you?"

Hannah cleared her throat. "I'm not sure. In the chest, I think."

"She's hamburger," he growled.

"Do you think she has a calf?"

"If she does it'll be her last. Come on, honey, I'll carry you to the house."

"No, I can... Ahhh!"

"What?"

She was panting now. "I guess I hurt my ankle."

"Geez, Hannah, I'm sorry." He eased his arms under her. "Hold on to my neck."

"No, really I—"

"What? You want to carry *me*?"

She laughed, but the sound was raspy.

"Easy, honey. Easy," he said. "Come on."

"No, really!"

"Really, what?" he asked, straightening with her in his arms. But when his gaze caught hers, he saw there were tears in her eyes, sparkling there, not yet set loose. "Hannah." He breathed her name.

"Please," she murmured. "It's my job. I said I could do it, and I..." She drew a catchy breath. "It's important that I do."

He'd thought he'd seen stubbornness before. When Nate was eight years old he'd insisted he could ride Cranky's first calf. It took him twelve tries. By the time he was finished, his arms were nicked up like a distressed end table, and his face had sported more colors than an artist's palette, but he'd ridden the calf.

"You're saying you won't be happy until you've checked the stock?" he asked.

Mere inches separated their faces. Such proximity did nasty things to his blood pressure.

"This is the first job I've ever had." Her words were very soft, like a child's admission of some secret sin that the whole world already knew. To laugh at her would certainly be criminal.

"Really?" he asked.

She nodded.

"Then you'd better see it through," he said, and carried her away from the house.

"I can walk."

"No, you can't." He proceeded to make a round of the pasture with her in his arms. Not far from where she'd been struck, they found Cranky hovering over her firstborn. The calf was on its feet but shaking with cold.

"Shouldn't we put them in the barn?" Hannah asked.

"I'll get you in the house, then come back and take care of that."

"But…"

It was a mistake to glance into her eyes, for they were too wide and too pleading.

"Of course, I could use some help," he said.

He carried her to the gate that stood between the newborn yard and the pregnant heifer pasture. Setting her gingerly on her feet, he backed up a couple careful paces.

"You okay?"

"I'm fine."

"All right. Make sure no cows go in or out until I get back. I'm going to be carrying baby, so Cranky might be a little testy."

"I noticed she had a propensity toward that."

He almost reached out and touched her cheek to assure himself she was all right, but he stopped himself just in time.

"Just make sure you keep the gate between you and the cow," he said.

"You can count on it."

The rain had let up a little by the time he reached Cranky and the baby. Talking all the while, Ty approached the two slowly, then bent, never taking his gaze from the cow, and lifted the calf into his arms. Being careful to keep the newborn between himself and the mother, he backed slowly toward the barn. The cow followed with worried grunts and snuffled warnings, but finally they were through the gate.

Placing the baby down on the deep bedding of straw beneath the roof, Ty backed away and returned to Hannah.

"Good job," he said.

"Yeah." She smiled tentatively. "I can stand by a fence with the best of them," she said, and eased the gate shut.

"You did good," he insisted, and because he couldn't help himself, he bent and lifted her into his arms again.

She opened her mouth to protest, but he shushed her.

"Don't bother arguing," he said. "I do this for everyone."

"Really?"

Her face was very close to his. He could smell the sweet freshness of her shampoo but couldn't quite place it. Lemon? Papaya? Something that spoke of wealth and warmth, not of cow yards and twisted ankles. How long would she be here?

She cleared her throat. He felt her tension against his arms. "I suppose you carried Howard around just like this?" she asked.

It was difficult to even recall the old cowhand's leathery face when she was near. "You bet," he said. "All the time. It was in our contract. And he weighed more. 'Bout four inches shorter and fifty pounds heavier. You should gain some weight."

"Trying to make me look like Howard?" she asked.

"It'd be better for my blood pressure." He snorted. "Can you get the door?"

She did so with some difficulty, opening the barn door far enough to allow them to squeeze through.

They made a quick trip between the cattle stalls, then through the horse barn. All was quiet.

By the time they reached the house, Ty was feeling the strain on his back and arms.

"Door," he said.

She opened it with an ease borne of practice.

He strode quickly across the linoleum. "You know what I said about gaining weight? I changed my mind," he admitted, and bending, deposited her carefully on the couch. But when she was settled there, he found it impossible to draw away immediately.

"Here." He knelt near her feet. "Let me get those boots off."

"I can do it."

"Lie back," he ordered.

She did so. "I feel like an idiot."

"We all get trampled on once in a while," he said, reminding them both of his story about Cranky I.

He eased off her left boot.

She winced a little. "At least you didn't laugh," she said.

No, laughter had been the furthest thing from his mind. The panic had momentarily drowned his sense of humor. "How does it feel?"

"Fine."

"You lie," he said, and slipped off her other boot.

After depositing them in the hallway, he returned to her side.

"Want some pillows?"

"Really, you don't have to—"

But he turned away, returning in a few minutes with a trio of pillows and an ice pack. After removing her coat and covering her with a blanket, he propped her up, then moved back down to her feet.

"We're gonna have to get that sock off."

"Eventually," she said.

"Now."

"Are you always so bossy?"

"Sometimes I'm worse."

"I'm sure if I just rest it'll be fine in the morning."

"Or maybe it'll be swollen up like an eggplant."

"Eggplant?"

"Fat and purple."

"That'd be bad."

"Yeah." Setting his hands to her ankle, he paused with a scowl. "This could be ugly," he warned.

"You're telling me," she said. "I didn't shave my legs today."

"I'll try to hide my horror. Ready?"

She nodded.

In the end it wasn't as bad as he had feared. She hissed an inhalation between her teeth as he eased her sock off, but other than that, she remained silent.

The ankle was slightly swollen but not discolored.

"You must have twisted it when you fell," he said, fingering the swelling. "I'll get you something for the pain."

He was gone for several minutes. Hannah could hear him rummaging around in the kitchen. But soon he was back, carrying two mugs of hot chocolate and an assortment of other stuff.

She swallowed the pills he gave her and sipped the chocolate.

Tyrel drew up a chair next to her.

"I think we should ice it and bandage it," he said. "Unless you want to go straight to the doctor."

"The doctor?" She laughed. "It's nothing."

His gaze held hers. "Every time I think I've got a loop on you, you throw me," he said. "Surely Daddy wouldn't be happy if he knew his little girl were injured and unattended."

For a moment, she considered telling him that Daddy had begged her to stay at The Lone Oak. But her pride stopped her. "I'm not as delicate as you think."

"Delicate?" he said, feeling breathless. "Sometimes I think you could whip me and Nate with nothing more than the sharp edge of your tongue. Then sometimes..." He shrugged. "You're the kind to make a man wonder, Hannah Nelson."

She glanced at her mug. "I used to ride a horse called Sargeant Pepper. He could clear six feet without breaking a sweat. But sometimes he'd get sloppy, and the thing about Sarge was, he didn't care if he fell. Shelby used to call him The Tank."

Tyrel was watching her very closely, as if absorbing every word. She shouldn't speak of her past, she knew, shouldn't trust him. After all, her life was in danger. Not to mention her heart. But he seemed so safe, so comforting, so alluring that it all but left her speechless.

"Anyway, we'd made it to the triple bars. He was jumping strong. But he didn't get quite enough lift. We came down together, but he got to be on top." She picked absently at a loose thread in the blanket.

"So what happened?"

"I fractured my wrist. Daddy insisted I spend a few days in the hospital, and then he bought me a new Porsche."

"A step up from the Rabbit," he said.

"Yes. He bought me a Porsche and begged me not to ride again."

"And did you?"

She shrugged as if it didn't matter. But suddenly it did. All her life had come down to money and bribes, it seemed. And for the first time she understood what her father had meant in his letter. Life wasn't made up of things and possessions, but of effort and achievements. Achievements she'd never achieved.

"I rode some," she said. "But I had other things to do."

"Like?"

"Buff my toenails." She tried to smile, but it didn't quite work. "Shelby said if I didn't want to try he didn't need me there." She paused. The square of the window was absolutely black. "He was never impressed with either my money or my name. He said he didn't need anyone who didn't have the heart."

"Heart?" Tyrel's voice was nothing more than a warm murmur. "I've never known anyone with more heart than you, Hannah."

Suddenly she wished he would kiss her, would pull her into his arms and tell her she was worthwhile, strong, wonderful, sexy, smart. Right now, just hearing him say she had good diction might ease her mind.

"Well…" He cleared his throat after an eternity of silence. "I'll bandage that ankle."

She considered arguing, but it hardly seemed worth the effort.

Rising from his chair, he retrieved an Ace bandage from the floor. Then, lifting her legs, he scooted under her feet. His hands were very warm on her ankle, and his thigh, beneath the pad of her foot, felt as firm and warm as a stallion's chest. He wrapped her ankle with efficiency and care, and despite her hopes, the job was soon finished.

"Did you do that for Howard, too?" she asked, feeling breathless and silly.

"Sure," he said, "but you've got nicer...everything."

Their gazes caught.

"Well, I'll, uh...get you to bed."

She nodded, though she wasn't the least bit tired.

In a moment he lifted her in his arms again. The stairs creaked beneath their combined weight. He pressed her door open with his elbow. On the bed, Sean arched his back, then slunk away.

Ty deposited her gently against the rumpled blankets, but he didn't immediately draw his hands away. "Hannah..."

She stared at him, lost in a hundred thoughts she should not be allowing. "Yes?" The single word sounded uncertain, as though it wasn't sure if it were a question or an answer to something that had not yet been asked.

Ty drew a deep breath, then bending closer, swept a few strands of hair from her brow and kissed her forehead. "Sleep well," he said and turned away.

"Ty." His name came to her lips without her permission.

He turned in the doorway, his expression solemn, his body tense.

A thousand errant words flashed through her mind. *Stay with me, Ty. I love you, Ty.*

She banished them all. "Did you do that for Howard?" she asked. He looked bewildered. She felt like an idiot, knowing she was only trying to delay his inevitable departure. "Kiss him?" she whispered.

His grin was like warm brandy, slow, exhilarating. "Sleep

in,'' he said, and turning, pulled the door nearly closed behind him.

TY WOKE JUST AFTER six o'clock. Three calves had been born during the night. He'd spent time with each, iodining their navels, administering vitamin A shots. He should be tired. And yet his bed held little appeal. Not when *she* wasn't there with him.

Shaking his head, Tyrel banished the thought and dressed himself in jeans, T-shirt and a long-sleeved flannel shirt. Within minutes he was in the hallway, but despite his better judgment, he couldn't quite force himself past her door.

Knocking on the wall, he quietly called her name.

No answer.

''Hannah,'' he said again, and opening the door a crack, peeked inside. The bed was empty except for the one-and-a-half-eared cat who arched his back and made an unreceptive noise low in his throat.

Closing the door, Ty hurried down the stairs and into the kitchen.

''Where's Hannah?''

Two faces turned toward him. Pansy's wrinkled like a catcher's mitt, Nate's already grinning.

''She already left,'' Pansy groused. ''With nothing but an orange between her and starvation.''

''Left?'' Ty asked. Panic tasted bitter.

Nate laughed. ''Geez, brother, have some pride. She didn't skip the country. She just went out to the barn.''

Ty scowled and ran his fingers through his hair. ''How'd she look?'' he asked.

Nate's expression brightened even more as he shrugged. ''I don't know. Kind of like a blond Cindy Crawford.''

Ty made a noise that sounded surprisingly like the cat's. ''Was she limping?''

''Limping?'' Pansy and Nate said together.

Nate's expression was happier than ever. ''What the...''

He glanced at the minuscule cook, checked his profanity and continued. "...*heck* did you do to her?"

"It's none of your business," Ty said, and hurried outside. He found her in the horse barn, just peeling Nate's loop from the roping dummy. Leaning against the wall behind him, he watched her for a moment.

She'd pulled her hair into a flaxen ponytail that stuck out of the hole in the back of her cap. The word *Pioneer* was written across the crown. Her legs, encased in pale denim, looked slim and endless, and her torso was hugged by one of Howard's old shirts. It was Western cut, with little peaks on each pectoral. The peaks reached nearly to her nipples, and at the end of each peak was a pearl-toned snap. God help him!

"I thought you were going to sleep in," he said.

She looked up with a gasp. "Oh! No." She drew a deep breath. "I wasn't tired."

Pushing himself off the wall, he took a few strides toward her. "You should be off that ankle."

She cleared her throat and coiled her lariat. Never in his life had he seen a messier job done of it. "It's fine now," she said, and glanced up at him.

"Yeah?" It was absolutely the only word he could think of to say when she looked at him like that.

"Yes."

There was silence after that clever exchange.

"Listen," He broke the quiet with too much volume and felt foolish because of it. "We'll be taking Houdini into the Valley today for the stock show. I was wondering..." *Don't clear your throat, don't scrape your boot around in the dust, and for God's sake, don't blush like some half-witted hayseed,* he warned himself. "I was wondering if you'd like to come along," he said.

"Well, I—"

"I could use the help," he said quickly, then slowed his words and his breathing. "We'd be back tomorrow."

"I'd better stay here and keep an eye on the stock."

"Nate said he wanted to." It was a blatant lie. And not a good one. Nate might be a fair hand with the cows and a damn fine headin' partner, but he wasn't the kind to miss a day in town. "He said he'd like you to go instead of him. You may think showing a bull is all glamour and glory. But it ain't going to get me on 'Lifestyles of the Rich and Famous.'" He tried a smile to go with his clever wit. Geez, he was sad. And desperate. Desperate to be near her. To speak to her. To hear his name on her lips.

She lifted the rope. "But I should—"

He interrupted her again. "You could bring your lariat. In fact, they might have some roping demonstrations. You could pick up a few pointers."

"Well…" She paused. He held his breath like a child awaiting a lollipop. "I guess if you don't mind."

"Mind?" He almost choked on the word, but caught a draft of pride and lowered his tone an octave. "No. I don't mind. Be ready about three o'clock. Okay?"

Turning, it was all he could do not to click his heels as he left the barn.

HANNAH ENTERED the kitchen at exactly three o'clock.

Nate whistled. Ty turned toward her, holding his breath and hoping he wouldn't start hyperventilating again when his gaze settled on her.

Howard's shirt had been bad enough, but the salmon-colored cable knit that hugged her now was worse.

"I, uh…" She scooped back a few strands of hair that had come loose. She'd pulled it into some kind of unfathomable knot at the base of her neck—a style that might be appropriate for show jumping, or perhaps a coronation.

He could imagine her with a tiara. Who the hell was she?

"I've never been to a stock show," she said. "Do I look all right?"

"Yeah, I think you look all right," Nate said. "What do you think, Ty? She look all right to you?"

Wasn't it bad enough that his brain went limp every time

she walked into the room? Did Nate always have to be there to narrate his every problem? "You look fine," Ty said, and Nate laughed.

"Well, you two better be on your way. I told ol' Houdini there'd be women at the show, and he's all hepped up to go. Don't want him to tear the trailer apart."

"You ready?" Ty asked her.

"I'll just get my suitcase," she said, and turning, reappeared in a moment with the same leather bag he'd watched her tote through the snow while wearing nothing but a towel and a glare.

"Wow!" Nate said, staring at the gargantuan thing.

"That's what I said the first time I saw her…*it!*" Ty corrected.

Hannah's gaze met his. Silence ruled the world.

Ty cleared his throat. "We're off," he said, and taking the suitcase from her, practically ran for the door before he could hear Nate's inane lyrics float after him.

10

"WHAT DO YOU MEAN it's the best you can do?" Ty asked.

The teenager behind the counter looked beyond bored. In fact, in a stupor to be totally accurate. His head had been shaved some days before. Only a shadow of hair showed on his scalp. There was a silver hoop through his right ear. A chain ran from it to his nostril.

Apparently the twenty-first century had arrived in North Dakota. Tyrel was not the least bit surprised to learn he wasn't prepared for it.

"The stock show thing's a big deal around here," the boy said, sounding bored. "You should have made reservations early, man."

"I did make—" Ty began, then took a deep breath and stopped. "Just give me my key."

It was delivered with less than good grace.

Ty found Hannah just as she was leaving the ladies' rest room. He cleared his throat. "We've got a small problem."

"It's not Houdini!"

"No." The bull was still in the trailer. After seeing how busy Valley Green was, they'd decided they'd best secure their own lodging first. "Houdini's fine. It's just..." He had seen her temper and really didn't care to have it displayed here in the hallway of the Super 8. Especially now, when they were just beginning to forge a fragile peace between them. "I couldn't get two rooms."

She stared at him, her brows slightly raised.

"I know this sounds like a cheap romance novel, but I

swear I didn't mean to do this. Nate and I were planning to come together, so we thought we might as well share a room, seeing as how Nate's hardly ever around anyway. So I thought, hell, why pay extra,'' he blathered, feeling panicked. "Anyhow, we reserved a room with two double beds. But now the kid at the desk says we only have one single. And I know this sounds like some kind of sleazy ploy, but I swear to God, I didn't expect—''

"So we only have one room?'' Her voice was soft. A bad sign. Ty tensed.

"'Fraid so.''

"With one bed?''

He cleared his throat. "One *twin* bed.''

He all but winced as he waited for her temper to blow. But instead, she lifted one shoulder and reached for the key.

"This place is packed like Macy's on sale day,'' she said. "If I scream someone's sure to hear me.''

He stared at her in dumbfounded silence.

The corner of a grin lifted her apricot lips. He narrowed his eyes, suspicious.

"What are you saying?''

She laughed, actually laughed. "I'm saying, I think I can trust you, Mr. Fox,'' she declared, and turning, headed for the stairs.

He felt as though he'd entered the twilight zone, and the kid at the front desk had been the gatekeeper.

Hannah opened their room door and stepped inside. Ty followed, carrying her gargantuan suitcase and his own duffel bag. He stood by the wall like a lost child.

"So you're okay with this?'' he asked, knowing he was acting like a fool, but desperately wondering what had happened to the woman who said she'd rather be fricasseed and served with cheap wine than spend a minute in his company. Had she, perhaps, come to care for him, or did she think she had him so cowed, he wouldn't possibly try anything out of line? The idea, he realized, had some merit. And yet he wasn't at all certain he had the discipline to spend a chaste *minute* in her company, much less a whole night!

"Sure. I'm okay with this," she said, taking her luggage from him and wrestling it onto a foldout stand made just for that purpose. "I've seen *It Happened One Night.*"

"It Happened One Night?" He frantically searched his mind. But if he had ever seen that movie, he couldn't remember it. He could only hope that it was a film where the couple had made frantic, passionate love from dusk to dawn, but somehow he doubted it.

"Clark Gable and Claudette Colbert," she explained. "They hung a blanket between them. It was perfectly respectable."

"A blanket," he said. Just being in the same hotel room with her was making his fingernails sweat. "I get kind of cold at night. 'Fraid there might not be any blankets to spare." To his surprise, she laughed at him as she unbuckled her suitcase. It opened in a moment and he caught a glimpse of a skimpy bit of lace.

"We'd best see to Houdini," she said.

He tried to agree, but his tongue was stuck to the roof of his mouth and his gaze glued to the lacy scrap that would cover some part of her anatomy that he'd dreamed of a thousand times.

She closed her suitcase and cleared her throat. "Tyrel?"

"Yeah," he said, breaking from his reverie, and feeling foolishly certain that his eyeballs had popped out like Roger Rabbit's. "Yeah, you're right. Just…just come on down when you're ready," he said, then fled like a panicked colt.

IT WAS A SHORT DRIVE from the hotel to the show grounds. In a matter of minutes, the paperwork was done and Ty had Houdini secured to a metal ring set in a wall at the end of a row of other Anguses.

Hannah eyed the others. Shiny black and immaculately clean, they looked like so many preppy students parked beside a grungy teenager. But Houdini seemed oblivious to his short-coming, and eyed them like a king amongst peasantry.

"I got my work cut out for me, don't I?" Ty said, wincing a little as he perused his only entry.

"Are you telling me you want him to look like them?" Hannah asked, nodding toward the preppy row of blacks.

"Like that only better," Ty corrected.

"Then I think you're going to need my help."

"Listen, Hannah." He smiled and her heart thwopped painfully in her chest. How on earth was she going to keep from throwing herself at him before they returned home? Maybe Claudette Colbert could manage a chaste night, but she'd only had to resist Clark Gable, who, by the way, had big ears. Even Tyrel's ears were sexy. "I really didn't bring you here to get more work out of you. Just go relax. Rest that ankle. Have a look around."

"And leave you here with mud boy?" she asked. Perhaps she should be honest, admit her weakness. But the thought of telling him that she wanted nothing more than to help him wash manure off a bovine's rump was more than her rumpled pride could endure. "Believe me, he needs a woman's touch," she said.

"Don't we all?"

His tone was as soft and tough as chamois, making her breath stop and her heart go wild.

"Sorry," he said. "I didn't mean that. Go have a good time, Hannah. You don't want to get your good clothes dirty."

"They're not good."

"They look good," he said, then cleared his throat and grinned sheepishly as if he wished he could draw the words back. "Go on, Hannah, before I make a complete fool of myself."

She stared at him. Could it be he really cared about her? Could it be his concern for her wasn't just driven by hormones or an empty wallet, as her past relationships had been?

"I'm helping you," she said.

He started to protest, but she stopped him, and finally he turned away. She watched him bend to rummage about in a large, wooden trunk he'd already carried in. His jeans stretched tight over his muscled backside. In many ways, it was far more intriguing even than his ears.

"Here. You can wear these," he said, straightening. She snapped her gaze from his behind to the rolled-up garment in his hand.

Their fingers brushed as she reached for it. Her breath caught in her throat, but she forced herself to ignore it and keep her gaze on the overalls. "Let me guess. Howard's?" she asked. The embroidered name near the collar proved her right.

"Believe me, we'll both be safer once you're in them." His voice was husky.

She had intended to refuse, but the sound of his husky voice was muddling her thinking, and in a moment she had removed her half boots and was pulling up the lightweight overalls.

"This is a bad sign," she said, pulling up the rusty zipper with some difficulty. "They fit."

He was silent for a moment as he stared at her. But he yanked his gaze away in an instant. "I knew Howard a long time. Those are from his younger days. He didn't age real pretty."

"Maybe it's the life-style."

"I take that personally," he said, then as she slipped into her suede boots, he produced a pair of large overboots.

She raised her brows. "Yours?" she asked.

"No." One corner of his lips lifted into a satyr's grin. "My rubbers are much, much bigger."

A FEW HOURS LATER, Houdini was a new bull. He'd been bathed, shaved, brushed and primped.

Hannah, on the other hand, had been hosed down, worn-out, butted and trampled on. And never had she had more fun.

"Well, Howard," Ty said. He'd taken to calling her that sometime before, after an acquaintance of Ty's had mistaken her from behind and greeted her as Howard. "I feel like I've been run over by a steam shovel. Bed will feel like heaven."

Bed!

Their gazes met. They were standing very close, and for one frantic second, she hoped he would kiss her, right there and then in front of the cows and everything.

"Ty!" someone called, shattering the moment.

Tyrel turned away with an effort. "Walt," he said.

Hannah steadied herself, trying to find her equilibrium.

"Hey. Didn't know if I'd see you here or not," said the newcomer. His belly was as big as an apple barrel, testing the buttons on his striped shirt.

"Yeah, we brought Houdini here," Ty said, nodding toward the Angus.

"Oh," Walt said, but he didn't look at the bull. Instead, his gaze slipped from Hannah's face to her name tag. "Howard," he said. "You're looking good."

For a moment she was stymied. Her world had turned upside down. She shouldn't be grooming a bull. She shouldn't be seen wearing powder blue overalls and someone's discarded baseball cap. And she certainly shouldn't be enjoying it. But her cheeks were sore from laughing and the thought of spending a night with Tyrel Fox made her feel as though her hormones were exploding. So she stuck out her hand, swaggered a little, and said in her best baritone, "Good to see you again, Walt."

"I THOUGHT OLD WALT was going to bust a gut," Tyrel said, pushing aside his plate and sipping his coffee. He may be an idiot, but he wasn't fool enough to share the wine Hannah had ordered with her shrimp. Tonight was going to be trying enough without confusing the issue with alcohol. Just helping her from her wet overalls had nearly been more than his wilt-ing self-control could handle.

She glanced across the dining table as she set her flute aside. It was constantly amazing to him how her eyes could show a thousand emotions without her luscious little mouth changing a whit. "I rather felt like Howard by the time I was done."

"I didn't think so."

The memory of him wrestling with Howard's rusty zipper snapped between them.

He froze, trying to change the subject, to pretend he hadn't spoken another inappropriate word. Geez! He had to think of something to say, to smooth over the moment. But nothing clever came to mind. Only the truth.

"It's not my fault," he said with resignation.

She stared at him with those unearthly blue eyes, and sud-denly there seemed little reason to pretend his stomach didn't knot and his wits didn't dissolve every time she was near.

"I don't mean to say such harebrained things to you, but my mind has turned to silage. It happened the first time I saw you in them white pants, standing in the slush beside that damned Rabbit." He shrugged, knowing he'd taken the final leap. But in truth, he'd leaped long ago, and she'd torn his heart to shreds. He had nothing to lose. Pride was overvalued anyway, he assured himself. "My wits haven't returned yet. So I'm warning you now, Hannah..." He stared into his cof-fee, then took another sip. "A blanket hung between us wouldn't do no more good than a red cape with a Spanish bull. If I were you I'd wear steel armor and knock me over the head with a baseball bat just to be on the safe side."

The truth lay between them like a live grenade.

She lowered her gaze to her wineglass, and for a moment he thought her hand trembled.

"And what if I don't want to be on the safe side?"

Her words were very soft, but he heard them. They curled

through his mind, then sparked through every nerve, setting his body on red alert.

"What?" he murmured, just in case he had been wrong. In case his own dreams had somehow deluded him.

"I think…" She paused as her long, slim fingers curled around the stem of the glass. "I think maybe I've been playing it safe all my life."

He tried to keep breathing. It was an abject failure. "There's something to be said for taking risks," he said. His voice sounded odd, he thought, as if he'd been kicked in the belly by a Clydesdale.

She cleared her throat and lifted her gaze to his. "Are you ready to go?"

"Yeah!" The word was two octaves too high for sure and far too eager. He tried again. "Yeah," he said, lowering his voice. "If you are."

He wouldn't have blamed her a bit if she'd laughed at him. But instead she smiled nervously. "Yes, I'm ready."

The drive to the hotel was absolutely quiet, the climb up the stairs the same. Hannah opened the door.

Ty closed it behind them, and then they stood in the dim light of the lamp. They gazed about the room as if another living soul wasn't doing the very same thing only inches away.

He could feel her tension, and took a deep breath in an attempt to relieve his own. "Listen, Hannah, I don't mean to twist your arm. I know I've been—"

But suddenly she was kissing him. His gut clenched and his mind did that little whirring thing it did when she so much as breathed. Now it reacted like a helicopter in full flight.

For a moment he just stood there like a bull-tromped clown, and then he slipped his hand around her waist and kissed her back. Feelings sizzled through him, sparking from one nerve ending to the next with lightning speed until his whole body was ablaze.

It was then that she drew away.

"Geez, woman, where'd you learn to kiss like that?" He barely managed the words, what with his mind whirring and his gut clenching, and his knees beginning to buckle.

"Colorado," she whispered, and kissed him again.

By the time she drew away this time his head felt light and the rest of his body very heavy. All this time she had seemed cool and aloof, and he had guessed those qualities had kept her away from men, but he wondered now if her sexual experience might well outdistance his own. Was that something he should apologize for, or should he just fall on his knees and beg her to teach him everything she knew? Or maybe he should just propose right now before she realized his own ineptitude.

"Listen, Hannah." His voice didn't sound so good. Kind of raspy and harsh and croaky. "It's not that I don't know what goes where or anything, but I'm kind of rusty, and I'd sure as hell hate to disappoint—"

But her kisses had slipped from his lips and fell in a hot rapid trail down his throat. Suddenly he realized his shirt had come open, and her hands were skimming down his abdomen like warm scented oil.

He sucked his breath in and tried to remember what he'd been saying. But damn if it hadn't blown completely from his mind, so he concentrated on keeping himself from tossing her to the bed and devouring her whole.

It was the most difficult thing he'd ever done in his life. But finally he allowed himself to slip the sweater over her head. Her slim arms stretched upward. Her hair was messed and her eyes were as bright as sapphires.

He found her eyes with his own. She pulled her shoulders in as if trying to hide herself, and suddenly he saw something in her eyes. Fear! Oh, God, it was fear! But of what? Sex? Intimacy? Him?

He let her sweater dangle in his fingers, took a deep breath, and tried to speak. But he couldn't, so he blew out the breath and tried again.

"If you're not sure of this, Hannah, it's not too late to stop."

No. Not too late. There were likely any number of insane asylums within hours of here. Couple of heavy-duty strait-jackets and he'd be perfectly safe.

"I don't want to quit," she whispered.

He canted his head slightly as his breathing started up again. "What'd you say?"

"I don't want to quit, but I'm still…" She paused. "It's been a long time for me."

"Long time." He touched her cheek. "For me, too," he said, and ran his fingers slowly down her arm.

"I mean a *really* long time." He felt a shiver run through her.

"Cold?" he asked.

She shook her head, but he didn't believe her. Taking her hand, he led her to the bed. Every instinct, every craving hormone in him begged him to hurry, but she was scared, and if there was ever anything he didn't want to mess up, it was this night with her.

He bent and drew back the covers. She sat down on the bed, kicked off her boots, and lay down on her side.

Tyrel watched her for a moment, then sat on the edge of the bed and pulled off his own boots. Turning then, he brushed his knuckles from her cheekbone to the corner of her mouth.

"You're sure?" he asked.

"I'm sure," she said, and reaching beneath his shirt, touched his chest.

He closed his eyes to the rush of feelings, and leaning forward, kissed her lips.

Her hand slipped down his abdomen. His muscles coiled beneath her fingers.

"Hard." She whispered the word against his lips.

"Yeah." His own voice sounded like a croak, and he realized foggily that he had no idea what she was talking about.

Her hand slipped around his side, urging him closer, and he gladly obliged until they were lying chest to chest, his half covered by a thin shirt and hers with nothing more substantial than a scrap of pink satin.

Pink satin with a tiny bow between her breasts. Holding his breath, he felt that bow, then slid his fingers higher to slip a narrow strap from her shoulder.

Leaning forward, he kissed that spot. She shivered against his caress. Reaching past her, he pulled the blankets over them.

Warmth and titillation surrounded them. She touched his chest with both hands, then spread them outward, over his shoulders, sweeping his shirt away. Her fingers felt like velvet against the muscles of his arms, and when his sleeves slipped off his hands, he lifted her fingers in his and kissed them softly.

He heard her catch her breath as he kissed each slender digit. She shivered as he slid his hands up her arms, and when he loosened her bra and kissed her breasts, she arched against him, her breath warm and soft against his hair.

The remainder of their clothing disappeared without his conscious knowledge and finally they lay stretched against each other with nothing between them but hard desire and aching need.

Her hand, soft and warm and tentative, slanted over the curve of his buttocks and onto his thigh. He held his breath as she brushed his erection.

"Do you have..." Her words paused, but her fingers did not. "A rubber?" she whispered.

He sucked air between his teeth and let his head fall back slightly as her fingers skimmed along the muscles of his belly. Feelings seared him like a windswept blaze, but he tried to concentrate on her words. "Rubber? No, I..." Her hands were like magic, setting him on fire. "I left them at the barn. Oh." He caught her hand with a shiver and pulled it gently upward before he exploded into a thousand scorched pieces. "You didn't mean that kind of rubber."

It took a Herculean effort to force himself to his feet. He carried his jeans around the bed and into the bathroom, and luckily he still had those condoms in his wallet.

Sweat had popped out on his forehead by the time he found one in the third compartment he searched.

Moments later, he slipped back in bed behind her. She was curled up with her back to him and looked very small and very fragile.

A thousand tender feelings flooded him. Pushing her hair aside, he gently kissed her neck. "You asleep?"

Hannah laughed. It sounded nervous to her own ears. "No."

He slid his hand down her arm. Warmth washed through her. She tried to relax. But it was all new and she had waited so long. His hand slipped onto her waist, over the curve of her hip. Against her will, she tensed.

"Hannah." He breathed her name. "If you want me to stop…"

"No!" She rolled quickly to her back and caught his gaze with her own. His eyes were dark, solemn. "No," she whispered. "I'm not frigid, Tyrel, I just don't know—"

"Frigid!"

She couldn't hold his gaze. "I'm not an ice princess," she whispered. "But I just—"

"I'm sorry about that stupid bet, Hannah. I never thought you frigid. I just thought you too good for me. It was my way of coping—"

"Too good for you?" She shook her head as feelings swamped her. Feelings of warmth and hope and everlasting. "All my life I've never fit in. Acting as if I was too good was a…a defense I suppose. But really…I've never been good enough."

"That's not true. You—"

She pressed her fingers gently to his lips, stopping his words.

"Look at you, Tyrel. Look at who you are. So good and kind and strong. Even on that first day, when I was acting like a house should come and fall on me, you took me in. And you're accomplished. You've made something of your life, with your ranch and your horses." She drew a deep breath. For the first time in her life she realized all her shortcomings. She could only hope he might want her anyway. "I'm not made of ice. I have feelings, Tyrel," she whispered. "Let me show you."

"Okay," he murmured, and ever so gently, kissed her lips.

She kissed him back with all the pounding emotion that raged through her. But a thousand other tempting places called to her. She moved lower, kissing each one, the hard slope of his chest, the slanting ribs, the rippled strength of his belly. Touching and feeling and kissing until his body was as tense as a bowstring, and he wrapped his arm around her to pull her beneath him.

Their gazes met, fire on fire, and then he was kissing her again, searing away any doubt she might have, kissing her ear, her neck, the tiny dell between her collarbone. She gripped the sheet beneath her in clawed fingers as his caresses moved lower, setting flame to her breasts, blazing a trail down her abdomen, nibbling at her belly button, her thighs.

She was hot and wet and impatient, writhing beneath him when he slid upward and braced an arm on either side of her body. She opened her eyes to find his.

"Not icy," he whispered, and slowly lowered himself onto her.

He was hot and hard and so sexy it stole her breath away. She welcomed his entry with a small gasp of pleasure.

They moved in tandem, slowly at first, tentatively.

But there was a tightness inside her.

"Hannah?" He drew back slightly, his expression quizzical, but now was hardly the time for a long-winded explanation, so she wrapped her legs around him and pulled him closer still.

"Please," she gasped.

Heaven's gates closed around Tyrel. He hissed in abject pleasure, and there was nothing he could do, nothing, but let the strength of her legs draw him in.

And suddenly they were pushing against each other with desperate need, rising and falling and gasping. Striving for satisfaction until they reached their final destination and with paired groans, fell over the summit and down into the soft dark folds of satiety.

Kissing her brow, Ty rolled onto his side. Her eyes were closed and she was breathing hard. He kissed her lips, her cheek, smoothed his hand down her arm and watched her fall asleep.

As for himself, sleep stayed far away. Instead, he lay in the dimness and studied her face, how the pale light shadowed and illumined. How her lashes lay like thistledown against her skin, how her breasts rose and fell as she breathed.

He was in love with her. Hell, he was crazy about her, and he didn't know the first thing about her, not even that she had been a virgin.

"HERE YOU GO, then," said the waitress. She was in her late forties, bleached blond, with eyes that suggested they had seen it all. "Coffee black as sin, two scrambled eggs and—" Her words stopped short as her gaze meandered off to the left.

"Hannah!"

Hannah turned at the sound of Ty's voice.

"You're up," she said, and despite every warning she had given herself, she felt herself blush.

"I was worried sick about you."

"Worried?" Hannah raised her gaze to his. Feelings like sunshine and laughter flooded through her as she remembered his every touch, his every word of the night before.

"What are you doing down here?" he asked, touching her cheek.

His top three buttons were still open and the rest were mismatched, setting his whole shirt askance. Apparently he had dressed in a hurry. The thought bumped up her heart rate.

"Housekeeping was busy," she explained. "I wanted to get you breakfast in bed."

"Breakfast in bed?" He all but whispered the words as he brushed his knuckles against her cheek. "Honey, all I want is you in my bed."

Her knees turned to pudding, her mind to oatmeal. Behind her, she heard the bleached waitress sigh.

Ty glanced up, cleared his throat, and grinned crookedly. "I'll, uh...I'll take that," he said. Leaning past Hannah, he picked up the cardboard tray with one hand and pressed the other to the small of her back, herding her toward their room.

Hannah all but swooned. Maybe they could skip the stock show. Maybe they could skip the rest of their lives and hole up in their room until—

From the corner of her eye, she saw a bearded man turn onto the stairs. Sharp memories ripped through her. A dark parking lot. Fear! She gasped and stopped dead in her tracks.

"Hannah, what is it?"

Her heart was galloping along like a racehorse in her chest as she stared at the stairway where the man had disappeared.

But it couldn't be him! They couldn't have found her here. No one knew where she was. No one except Daddy. But the memories of that terrible night haunted her. A dark-bearded face, short-cropped hair. Fear as bitter as gall.

"Hannah, what's wrong?"

"Nothing," she said, but the panic was still roiling. Jerking away, she ran for the door.

"Hannah!" She could hear him running behind her, but fear pushed her on, outside, into the parking lot.

From the corner of her eye she caught the movement of something shiny and red. Jerking around, she saw the old pickup bearing down on her. Fear turned to ice in her veins. Her own scream filled her head. Death swooped down on her.

But suddenly Ty slammed her from the side, knocking her out of the way. The pickup roared past. Tires squealed as it rounded the corner and raced out of sight.

"Hannah! Hannah!" Ty's voice drew her back to reality. But she could barely feel his hands on her skin. "Are you all right?"

"I—I think so." She managed to gain her feet, but her hands were shaking and her knees felt weak.

"Damn bastards!" he growled. "I'm gonna call the police! Be simple enough to describe that old truck."

"No!" She grabbed his sleeve with desperate strength. "Not the police!"

11

IT HAD BEEN OVER A WEEK since the stock show. Despite Hannah's state of obvious distress after the scene with the red truck, she had insisted Tyrel exhibit Houdini. The bull had had a decent showing, taking reserve champion, despite his handler's distraction.

Back at The Lone Oak now, Tyrel sat on the fence and watched Hannah. It seemed as if a lifetime had passed since their night in Valley Green, since he'd kissed her, held her, made love to her. And since that time the woman she'd become had disappeared, drawing back into the woman she had been—haughty, distant, cool. She had, for the most part, acted as if nothing had happened between them, as if she hadn't stolen his heart, as if she hadn't been moved by the magic that had touched them both.

There were a thousand things he wanted to ask her. Why hadn't she told him she was a virgin? What had frightened her so? Who the hell was she? A princess, an heiress, a thief? Why was she here, and why had she panicked when he'd suggested involving the police? Frustrated by her silence as much as by his own swirling feelings, he had called his father and insisted on learning some facts.

But the old man, cagey as ever, had said all Ty needed to know was that she was the daughter of an old friend.

Ty, as usual in his conversations with his dad, had blown up and sworn he would turn Hannah out of The Lone Oak. After all, he had no intention of harboring a jewel thief.

When Robert Fox had finally overcome his laughter, he

assured Ty that Hannah Nelson may be many things, but she was *not* a jewel thief.

The conversation had done nothing but make Tyrel more frustrated. The days had dragged by with every second filled with thoughts of her in his arms, in his bed, in his life.

But now the three weeks prescribed by the roping bet were past. She sat upon Nathan's palomino, twirling a rope above her head in order to prove herself his equal in the arena as well as everywhere else.

But he would gladly admit it. Hell, he'd say she was far superior on every damn front if she would just open up, let him in to that secret place in her heart—that place he would have sworn he had been for a few euphoric hours.

The bet was that she could rope one out of the first three steers that came out of the chute, but she'd shagged a bunch more animals in there. They milled behind the metal panels now, their horns clicking against each other's as Nathan manned the release gate.

A large brindle animal stood in the narrow passage, his eyes wild.

"You ready, Hannah?" Nate called.

Bent slightly forward over the saddle horn, she looked as if she'd roped all her life, like a wild cowgirl who had been born astride and weaned with a piggin' string in her hand.

Feelings as hot as flame seared Ty. He loved her, and felt that painful knowledge rip through his heart.

She was tense now, ready. Her eyes were focused straight ahead, and in them he saw a glimpse of the woman he had made love to just days before. A vivacious, tenderhearted woman with fire and spirit.

"Ready?" Nate called again.

Ty knew she was. She was a tiger in a pussycat suit. Tougher than sin, softer than a sigh.

Ty watched her calm Lula as Nate reached forward and pulled a lever.

The gate burst open with a clang. The steer lunged ahead,

running flat-out. Hannah's mount charged after him. She was swinging fast, then tossed. But her aim was off a bit. The loop sailed through the air and caught one of the steer's horns. The beast careened to a halt, his head cocked sideways. The lasso fell to the earth.

Lula pranced and champed her bit, irritable at the failure.

"That's all right, honey," Nate called to Hannah who recoiled her rope and turned the mare back to the starting position.

The steers were unhappy with their confinement. They milled nervously, but finally Nate was able to chase another up to the narrow gate.

"Ready?" he called again.

Lula pranced, tossing her flaxen mane. Hannah waited for her to settle, then nodded.

Again the gate swung open. The steer burst free. Hannah leaned into the mare's movement, already swinging. Ten strides into the arena, she tossed the loop. It sailed like magic through the air and landed, perfect as morning, over the steers wide horns.

Nate hooted with delight. Climbing onto the big, metal gate, he whipped off his hat and waved a wild salute to Hannah as he yelled again.

Inside the small pen, the steers lunged wildly against each other. Panicked by the close confines and the bursting noise, they jostled and milled, banging the unlatched gate that Nate was perched on. As the gate swung wide, the steers burst through the narrow opening, scrambling and bawling.

In horror, Ty watched as Nate teetered on the upper rung, and then, able to hold on no longer, he fell, glancing off a steer's bony hip before hitting the mud with a hard jolt. Ty and Hannah rushed over to Nate's side.

"You all right?" Ty asked, his voice tense with worry. Ty had been in a hell of a mood for the past week.

Nate's news wasn't likely to improve it.

"How DOES IT FEEL?" Ty asked.

"Feels like a broken leg," Nate said, settling his new cast under the table and grinning shakily. The morphine had begun to wear off even before they'd stopped for lunch on their way home from the hospital. "Looks like I won't be doing much two-stepping for a while."

"Or chores." Ty scowled.

"Yeah, it's a shame." Nate's grin steadied. "Looks like I'll have to sit around and write songs and play the guitar."

Ty winced as he set his cup to his lips. He'd asked for black coffee, not boiled tar. "What the hell were you thinking?" he asked, narrowing his eyes for the steam that rolled up from his dark brew.

"It was my fault," Hannah said. Ty and Nate turned to her in unison. She still looked scared, Ty noticed, but her color was better. "I should have latched the gate."

"No—" Both men spoke at once, but Ty glared down his brother, who grinned back.

"Nate knows better than to goof around with them steers. We only keep them for roping. Half of them are wild, and the other half are plain stupid."

"I'm sorry." Her apology was very soft.

Something ripped in Ty's heart. The truth was, he'd rather have her steaming at him in haughty indignation than to have her look so shaken. Every instinct in him told him to wrap her in his arms, but his foolishness had to end somewhere.

Nate shrugged at Hannah's reaction and turning, spotted a newspaper on the chair by the next table.

After glancing at it for a moment, he scrambled awkwardly sideways and picked it up. "Hey." He scowled at the front page. "Didn't you say it was a red pickup that almost ran Hannah down?"

"Yeah," Ty said, straightening.

"Must be a rash of stupid red pickup drivers," Nate continued. "'Cuz look. Says here Peter Dicks was sued for bust-ing down some old lady's mailbox on April twelfth.'' He glanced up. ''Wasn't that the day you were in town?''

Ty scowled. ''Peter Dicks. Bill's kid? You mean he was the son of a bitch that nearly killed us?''

''Looks like it. Works at the plant here in town now.'' Nate snorted. ''Always was dumber than a pile of rocks.''

''And drunk half the time. I should—''

''Can I…can I see that?'' Hannah asked. She felt faint and her hand shook slightly when she reached across the table for the newspaper. Staring at the picture of the man and the pickup, she scrambled for reality. It was a distinctive vehicle, an antique probably, restored to a bright cherry finish with big rounded fenders and acres of shining chrome. Moving her gaze from the photo, she skimmed the article, then stared at the picture again. The chances against there being another vehicle like this in such a small town were astronomical. ''So this Peter Dicks—he's local?'' she asked, her heart beating like running hooves.

''Did you say local or loco?'' Nate asked.

''Yeah.'' Ty was watching her closely. She could feel the intensity of his gaze on her face. ''He's local. He was a couple years behind me in school. Moved off the farm a while back. Why?''

Silence echoed around her.

''So he's…'' She paused, knowing she'd look nuttier than a fruitcake if she asked what she wanted to. *Was Peter in the habit of hiring out as a hit man? Could he have been paid to kill her?* Even in her mind, the idea sounded like lunacy. She almost laughed out loud with her rampaging relief. ''He's…so what's he like?'' she asked, still grasping at straws.

''Stupid,'' Nate said, distracted now, since their meals had arrived.

''Reckless,'' Ty said, still watching her, his eyes narrowed. ''He's always been reckless.''

''So it was just an accident,'' she said, and knew without

a doubt that she was right. All her worry had been for nothing.

"What?"

She glanced up and met Ty's gaze. His expression was solemn, his eyes worried. Her heart turned over. The past few days had been horrible. Trying to figure out what to do. Trying to convince herself that she was safe. That *Ty* was safe. That just knowing her hadn't put his life in jeopardy.

"It was just an accident," she said, her voice breaking with the painful relief of tension. The man she'd seen in the hotel had borne a passing resemblance to the person who had attacked her in LA. So? Half the American male population did. But she'd panicked, run outside, and nearly gotten squashed by a passing pickup truck. It sounded as ridiculous as a country-and-western song. Too ridiculous to be anything but the truth. She felt suddenly giddy and couldn't help but throw her arms around Ty, hugging him close, closing her eyes against his chest.

"Hannah." He murmured her name.

She drew away with a laugh.

"What's going on?" Ty asked.

"Nothing. I was…" At a loss for words and slaphappy with relief. "I was just being silly. You know…" No, they didn't know. She could tell that by their expressions. And it was a good thing they didn't. "It just spooked me, that's all. There's been so much going on. Cranky mauling me. The pickup thing…" Both men stared at her. She laughed. Tyrel's life wasn't in danger. "But it was just an accident."

"Yeah, just an accident," Nate said, widening his eyes and clearly saying he had no idea what she was talking about. "Let's eat."

She turned nervously toward her salad. Realizing how loony she was behaving, she tried to act natural now.

"Dammit, Hannah," Ty said, his voice deep. "I want some answers."

"It's nothing." She felt her face flush and knew Ty had

run out of patience. "I just…I just had these wild imaginings that someone was out to get me. Silly." She tried a laugh. It didn't sound too bad. "Probably comes from living too long in—"

She stopped herself just in time.

Ty's gaze all but bore a hole in her.

"Colorado," she finished lamely.

His frown was not pretty.

Nate was watching them like a hawk as he chewed. "Hey," he said, his tone bright. "Now that we got that straightened out, why don't you team with Ty, Hannah?"

"What?" She turned rapidly toward him, grateful for any diversion. But what the devil was he talking about?

"I'm not going to be roping for a while," he said, pointing toward his cast with his fork. "Why don't you and Ty team rope together?"

Hannah blinked. Ty glowered. Nate grinned.

"It's a great idea, brother. She's a natural. Got an eye like an eagle. Lula hardly knows she's in the saddle. Well, hell!" He chewed for a moment. "You saw her. Oh—" He took a big slurp of milk. "You owe her one of them English saddles."

"And she owes me some answers," Ty growled.

"I'll do it." Hannah hadn't meant to say that, but she had to do something to turn the conversation. Ty was still glaring at her. She could feel his gaze on the heat of her face. "I mean, after all, it's my fault Nate can't rope."

"Who did you think was in that red pickup?" Tyrel asked.

She paused a moment, then forced a laugh as she turned to him. "No one. How would I know?"

"Then why were you so scared?"

"I told you. I was just being silly."

"Tell me the truth."

"The truth is, I'm not hurt and I'm ready to learn to team rope. Right now," she said, and standing up, made a quick retreat from the restaurant.

Four hours later Nate was parked on the couch with Pansy hovering over him like a grouchy hen.

Hannah recognized an old movie on the television. Her father had taken particular pride in that one. But the lines sounded rather stiff to her now.

"You must leave before it's too late," said the hero with resounding drama.

"Are you going to be okay?" Hannah asked Nate.

"Truth is, I don't think I can take much more of this dessert." He grinned around a mouthful of apple cobbler. "And TV and stuff. I'm dying to go shovel shit."

She left with a chuckle. A short while later she was cleaning stalls. Her relief had bordered on euphoria, but now the worries settled in. She'd been acting like a lunatic since the accident and though Tyrel had refrained from asking her any more questions on the way home, he was likely to want some—

"So what the hell was that all about?"

She turned with a start, only to find Tyrel watching her from the doorway. He was leaning up against the jamb, his expression angry, his face so alluring that for a moment she couldn't breathe.

His eyes were as dark as Colombian coffee and his lips strangely sensual against such a granite jaw. Despite her best efforts she could remember every moment of those lips against hers.

"You know, Hannah…" He straightened. "I'd think you could afford to give me one straight answer."

She marshaled her senses. "I don't know what you're talking about."

"Don't you?" He stepped restlessly into the stall. "So you've forgotten all about our night in town?"

She couldn't hold his gaze, and turned nervously back to her job, but he didn't go away. She could feel his attention on her face.

"Or didn't it mean anything to you?" he asked.

His voice was soft now, and she could do nothing but turn to him with her breath held and her heart in her throat.

"Is that what you think?" she murmured.

The barn was silent for a moment, then he said, "I don't know what to think. I don't know who you are. I don't know why you're here."

"I'm here for the job," she said, able to come up with no better answer with his hot attention turned on her. Able to give nothing away.

"Damn the job!" he swore. "Who are you?"

They stared at each other from inches apart.

"It doesn't matter who I am. It doesn't matter what my name is, or where I'm from. For the first time in my life, it doesn't matter. Don't you understand that? I'm just me."

A muscle jumped angrily in his jaw. "Well, it matters to me," he said. "I don't like to be lied to, to be used, manipulated like a—"

"I didn't use you."

He snorted. "You've been making me dance like a damn circus horse. It must've been fun watching me moon over you. Seeing me make a fool of myself as you spread your clever lies."

"I didn't—"

"Yeah? Where're you from, Hannah?"

She winced. She didn't like to lie, but neither did she like the thought of being murdered by a thug who called himself Lucky Lindy. And all because of one rude remark she'd made to the man. He *did* look like a toad. "Colorado," she said.

"What town?"

"Uh, Aspen."

"How long have you lived there?"

For a moment she tried to think of another lie, but finally her temper broke. "That's none of your business."

"Where'd you get that accent? What does your dad do? What's your real name?"

"Hannah…Nelson," she said defiantly.

"Yeah? Let me see your driver's license."

She drew a deep breath. "I will not."

"You must have one. You were driving. Is the Rabbit registered in your name?"

She paused. "Of course."

"Then who is Stone Gardner?"

She felt her jaw drop. Stone Gardner, her father's current protégé, and the former owner of the Rabbit. "You've been snooping around in my personal—"

"I wasn't snooping. The registration was in the glove compartment. I saw it when I, uh, hauled it out back." He sounded defensive and angry all at once. "So who is he, Hannah? Your husband?"

She gasped. "You think I'd sleep with you if—"

"But of course he's not your husband," he said, pacing the narrow confines of the stall, "because you were a virgin. But I didn't know that. You didn't see fit to share that little piece of information with me. So I'm wondering, who could this Stone Gardner be? It doesn't sound like a real name. More like something you'd see on the credits of a B movie." He took another step closer. "Who is he, Hannah?" he asked, grabbing her arm.

"That's none of your business either."

"Yeah?" He barked a harsh laugh. "According to you none of it's my business. Call me eccentric, but I like to know who I'm hiring. Hell, sometimes I even like to know who I'm sleeping with."

"Well, you can rest easy," she said, jerking her arm from his grasp. "Because it sure won't be me."

He stared at her, his eyes hard. "Damn straight," he said, storming out of the barn.

HANNAH LUNGED the leggy gray around the outdoor arena one more time. And one more time she glanced down the road as the filly circled at the end of the nylon line. Where was Tyrel? He'd been gone since before breakfast.

Not that she cared. He'd acted like a jerk two nights ago when she'd last talked to him, and he could damn well stay gone till hell thawed, which it seemed to be doing.

The sun felt warm on her face. The filly spooked from Sean who sat on the fence watching them with his eerie feline eyes. The lunge line drooped. Hannah snapped it, and the gray swerved away, allowing her handler's thoughts to drift again.

So what if Tyrel Fox was gone? So what if he was angry? She was Allissa Vandegard.

Or was she? Glancing over the top rail of the arena, she absorbed the wide, rolling country around her. There was something here. Something she'd never had before, something that touched her heart and quieted her soul. But what would it be without Tyrel? Without his smile? His laughter? The way he scowled into his pitch-black coffee as if it held the key to the world's problems.

She sighed.

The filly started, dragging her attention back to the business at hand. It was then that she noticed Ty's pickup turning into the yard.

Her heart rate bumped up a pace and her hands tightened on the nylon line. The filly fell to a walk, and Hannah allowed it as she struggled not to stare at the pickup. But she failed. In a moment the Jimmy rolled up beside the fence and stopped.

Hannah held her breath as Ty stepped out. He rounded the pickup, his muscular legs hugged by faded jeans, his torso wrapped in a soft flannel shirt, rolled up at the wrists, tucked in at his hard waist.

Without the slightest effort, she could remember how hard, how firm, how fine and sweet and...

"Do you have a minute?"

His voice sent a smoky curl down into her belly. She managed a nod, then unsnapped the line from the halter, setting the yearling free to cavort on her own.

Stepping to the passenger side of the pickup, Ty opened

the door. Hannah ducked between the rails and strode up to him.

Lying on the Navajo blanket that covered the bench seat, was an English saddle. It was German made, the leather soft as a glove, the seat fitted like a spoon.

Tyrel cleared his throat. "The fellow at the tack shop said it was top of the line." His eyes, when she dared look at them, were as soft as nightfall.

"They had *this* in Valley Green?"

"He, uh…he ordered it in for me."

Her throat tightened with emotion. "When?"

For a moment she thought he might not answer. Turning his head, he gazed past the arena to the hills beyond. "Well, hell, Hannah, I'm not as big a fool as I seem."

She didn't know what that meant, but her throat hurt and her eyes stung with unshed tears.

He glanced back at her. Their gazes caught.

"I knew you wasn't going to lose that bet. Not you. But it bought me a couple more weeks with you."

She swallowed. "Thank you." Her fingers lay against the soft-grained leather of the cantle.

"Yeah, well," he said, clearing his throat. "This is just for Maverick, you know. It don't mean you're going to get out of roping with me. If you still want to."

"I still want to."

He remained still for a moment, then finally nodded before reaching past her into the pickup and pulling out a package. "I got you a couple things." Their arms brushed as his straightened. Hannah held her breath. He paused for a moment, found his line of thought and pulled out a lariat. "Your own rope. A little lighter, three-eighths of an inch. Nate says you're real quick. But it'll improve your time maybe."

She loved him. Dear Lord! How had that happened?

He pulled his gaze away again. "And gloves. To keep your hands from…" He drew a heavy breath. "I may not know much about you, but I know you got nice soft hands." The words were barely whispered.

Memories of their one night together steamed through her. Touch, whispers, ecstasy. In his eyes, she saw the same thoughts.

He pulled himself out of the reverie. Yanking the tags off the gloves, he opened one pliable deer hide and held it for her. She slid her hand in. But he didn't draw away. Instead, he held it in both of his.

"I'm sorry." The words were very soft, his eyes as deep as forever. "You're right. Your name doesn't matter, Hannah. I'm just... I'm scared is what I am."

Scared? Him? She would have laughed if she didn't feel like crying. How many times had he saved her life both literally and figuratively?

"If you leave..." He glanced up, over her head. She watched a muscle tighten in his jaw. "*When* you leave—"

"And what if I don't?" She couldn't stop the words, couldn't help thinking the crazy thoughts that drowned her. Here was where she belonged. Right here.

"Don't say it." His eyes were intense, hard as shell, yet just as fragile. "Don't say it unless you mean it."

"I'm still here, aren't I?" she asked softly.

"Yeah." He cleared his throat, and turned his gaze away. "Yeah, you are," he said, his tone becoming brusque. "And I'm paying you good money. So you'd best get to work."

BUT WHAT THEY DID couldn't be called work. Oh, he tacked up Lula and Hannah mounted. But as soon as the first steer was let loose, he called her back.

"You gotta let the horse do the work," he said, motioning her to get down. "Lula here, she's been roping steers since before you was born. She knows just how it's done." Moving past Hannah, he threw up the stirrup and stripped off the saddle and pad. "Hop on up."

"Bareback?"

"Yeah, I'll give you a leg up."

"I'm not a great bareback rider."

"Really?" They were standing very close. So close she could feel his warmth, his emotion. "Then I'll ride with you. Make sure you don't fall off."

Her breathing escalated.

He cleared his throat. "It's the best way," he said seriously. "To feel the movement of the horse under you."

"Oh." Sure, she could believe that. Tandem bareback. Her heart was thumping.

He pulled his gaze away, and had no trouble mounting without the aid of stirrups. Getting Hannah on in front of him was a little trickier. But finally she was settled between his thighs.

She'd thought she'd felt his heat before. Now the warmth traveled up her body like wildfire.

"Yeah, this is, uh…this is better," he said, trapping her between his arms as he reached for the reins.

"Yeah."

"I mean, for teaching you how to gauge the steers."

"But, Ty," she said, not turning to look into his face, "there's no one to let them out."

"Oh." He cleared his throat as his arms tightened around her. "Well, maybe we'll just take a ride in the pasture then."

The afternoon sped by like a summer breeze. The sun was warm against Hannah's skin. Ty's voice was deep and low, evoking a thousand feelings that were only enhanced by his touch, the feel of his fingers against her hand, the warmth of his hard thighs behind hers.

By nightfall, she felt as if every nerve ending was made of kindling. She stood in the doorway of her bedroom with him, trying to douse the sparks.

"Good night, Hannah," he said.

No. Not good-night, her mind argued. Not good-night! Come in. Lock the door. Make love. But despite everything, she was still a Vandegard, and Vandegards did not beg.

"You could come in for a minute." That wasn't begging. Just a...suggestion.

He hesitated. "I'd better not."

"Please." Okay, that was begging a little. But what did he expect. He'd been driving her mad with his closeness all day. Now just the thought of him leaving made her want to fall at his feet.

Indecision showed on his face. Leaning forward, he kissed her lips.

Every awakened desire in her kissed him back. She slipped her hand quickly behind his neck, answering his caress.

"Her kiss is like summer lightning." The country lyrics drifted up the stairs, accented by the thumping of a cast and a foot.

Tyrel's expression was raw with desire when he pulled away.

"Good night," he said again, and turned stiffly away.

12

THE DAYS PASSED like water through a sieve. Ty could do nothing but let them go. Every moment with Hannah was a pleasant torment, every day one less he would have in the future, and yet he could not stop himself from being near her.

Allowing her to ride alone was nearly more than he could bear. But it would be difficult to teach her to team rope without doing so. And she was painfully determined to learn. She took his every criticism with sober-faced attention, nodding, leaning toward him, absorbing every word, like a soldier doing battle against failure.

There was no need for her to do this, no reason in the world she must learn to team rope. In his soul, he knew she was not what she pretended to be. And though he couldn't help but hope it didn't matter, that she would stay forever, his heart knew better. They were like fire and ice, a princess and a pauper.

The nights were long, for he would not make love to her. Not again. Not until she would trust him with her name, with her identity, with her heart. But during the day, he couldn't keep from touching her. Every facet of her fascinated him, every word, every glance.

"Yee-hah!" she yelled, copying the halloo that had earned Nate a broken leg. But it was adorable when she did it. Her eyes were as bright as crystal, her smile undimmed. "What's the time, Nate?" she yelled. Beneath her, Lula kept the lariat tight and the steer trapped between her and Ty's gelding.

"Seven-point-two seconds," Nate called from his place

near the chute. "You done good, honey. But if I was you I'd get myself a new partner."

Hannah laughed and Ty scowled. But he couldn't disagree. His mind was elsewhere—not on the roping, but on Hannah, on how she held the reins, how she turned just so in the saddle, how her slim thighs hugged the mare. And somehow, he couldn't help but envy her mount.

He was one sick puppy! Obsessed! Sleepless. He couldn't take it anymore. And he wasn't going to. If he was going to lose her, he was going to know why.

"TY." LORETTA FOX TURNED from the kitchen table in surprise. She'd gained a few pounds over the years, but she was still pretty. Delicate, some might think. Her sons knew better. "What are you doing here?"

"Can't the boy just stop by to see us sometimes?" asked her husband, rising from his chair, and going to the stove to pour himself another cup of dark coffee. At fifty-two, Robert Fox had pretty much perfected the art of irritating his firstborn son.

They were too much alike to get along. Ty knew that as well as anyone, but tonight he wouldn't let his temper get the best of him. Tonight he would get some answers.

"Do you want some coffee?" his mom asked.

"Yeah." Ty drew out a chair and sat down. "Thanks."

She poured him a cup. It slogged with tarlike reluctance from the spout. Tyrel had come by his taste through honest genetics. "Brownies?" she asked. "I just made them."

"No, thanks."

"Jell-O? I've got some left from Sunday."

"No."

"Oatmeal cookies? A little roast beef?" She was rummaging in the refrigerator now. "We've got some ham left over. Or—"

"Loretta," Robert said, "the boy probably just came by for some advice from his old man."

Tyrel took a sip of his coffee. It had the kick of a green broke mule. "Matter of fact I do need some advice," he said, turning toward his father.

"Yeah?" Robert settled his weight against the counter behind him. "Want to know how you can sell that ranch of yours and finally do something with that fancy education I paid for."

No, Tyrel thought. He wanted to know how he could have what his father had built with his mother. It was a realization he had never faced, and it stunned him now.

"Would it be so bad if I wanted to be like you, Dad?" he asked softly.

For a moment sheer surprise and something like pleasure showed on the older man's face. He hid it quickly away, but not before Tyrel had noticed. Something softened inside of him.

"Well..." Loretta looped the dish towel through the refrigerator handle. "I'll leave you two alone," she said, but as she passed Tyrel, she reached out to squeeze his arm. In her eyes there was an expression that said, "It's about damn time."

Had he been such an ingrate as all that?

"So..." Robert settled himself back into a chair across from Ty. "What do you need?"

"It's about Hannah."

"Hannah?" Robert's brows lifted in curiosity, but there was something else there. It almost looked like a sharp spark of hope.

"That's right."

"What about her?"

Ty scowled into his coffee, then back at his father. "I need to know who she is."

"Listen, son." He settled back into his chair. "I told you when this started that I couldn't tell you nothing about her. The money'll have to be enough consolation."

"I don't want the money," Ty said, his voice low.

"Listen, boy, I told you—"

"You didn't tell me I'd fall in love with her."

The words reverberated in the silence of the room, and then Robert smiled.

"So you think she's the one to settle you down—keep you on that no good piece of land of yours? Not that that's what I want," he hurried to add. "Farming's for fools, and ranching is worse."

"So you've said enough times."

"From what I heard she's not the farming type," Robert said, studying his son with narrowed eyes.

"Yeah, well, there's a lot more to her than meets the eye."

"I'll be damned. Old George thought that might be true."

"George?" Tyrel asked, his heart racing with the promise of any tidbit of information.

"George...Vandegard," Robert said, taking a sip of coffee and watching him carefully. "He's an old friend of mine."

"George...Vandegard...the movie director?" Ty asked.

"Yeah. That's the one."

HANNAH WAS TENSE. Tyrel could feel her thoughts as he watched her. She was nervous, worried, taut as a wound spring. Yet grace and elegance exuded from her, and he couldn't bear to lose her.

"Len Clemens and Toby Carter. Six-point-five seconds. That's the time to beat," called the announcer.

But Tyrel didn't care about the time to beat. He only cared about her. How long would she remain once she learned the truth? How long before she left?

"Are you ready?" Her eyes were as bright as morning, her smile like the flash of the sun through a gray bank of clouds.

No, he wasn't ready. He would never be ready. But he nodded. They rode side by side to the box behind the barrier.

In the stands, the crowd was silent. On the far side of the steer chute, Hannah tipped back her hat—the hat he had given her. Her gloved hands were steady on the reins.

"Ready?" The chute man glanced at Hannah. She nodded once. The gate sprang open. The steer charged out. Lula lunged after him, Hannah leaning over the horn.

Her throw was clean, catching both horns. She loped off with the steer moving along behind. Tyrel tossed his loop. It whipped in front of the steer's hind legs. Ty snapped up the slack, confining the animal between them.

"Six-point-two seconds, folks," called the announcer. "A new best time."

Ty and Hannah flipped their ropes off the steer, and exited the arena. They dismounted there, and suddenly Hannah was in his arms, hugging him with ferocious joy.

"We did good," she whispered.

"Yeah." His heart had stopped. "Yeah, you did good," he said. It was then that he saw the man in the sunglasses and red shirt. His stomach roiled. "Listen, Hannah..." He gently disengaged her arms. "I've got to go see a man about a horse. You stay and watch the others. Let me know how we stack up, huh?"

"Sure." Her exuberance was undiminished.

He turned away.

"Ty?"

He stopped at the sound of his name and turned back toward her.

"I..." She paused, grinned, and then continued with a shrug. "Thank you."

"Yeah," he said. Ty hitched Rowdy to the far side of the trailer.

"Tyrel Fox." A man's voice made him turn. The speaker was tall, graying, looking theatrical in a red fringed shirt, black jeans and cowboy hat that reminded him of Roy Rogers. He removed his sunglasses with one hand and reached out with the other. "So you're Robert's son."

Ty forced himself to clasp hands with the man. "Mr. Vandegard?" he said.

"Call me George." He smiled, and in the jut of his jaw,

Ty could see a hint of Hannah's stubborn tenacity. "This is Stone Gardner. Perhaps you've heard of him."

Not since reading the Rabbit's registration, Ty thought, then nodded to the younger man. He was dressed in a floor-length duster and a hat big enough to shade Arizona. Beneath the brim, he had the perfect nose borne of plastic surgery. His beard was close-cropped. "Stone," Ty said.

"So you've been taking care of my little girl," Vandegard said.

Ty drew back his hand. He felt sick to his stomach. "She really doesn't need taking care of."

"Stone here said the same thing after the incident in the parking lot," Vandegard said.

"She almost broke my arm," Stone added, sounding sullen.

Vandegard chuckled. "Be that as it may, she's still my little girl. And I've never seen her happier."

Ty held his gaze. "And what about when she learns the truth?" he asked. "Will she be happy then?"

Vandegard shook his head. "You don't understand. Allissa has such fire, such talent, but she never used it. She never *had* to use it. And her mother thought... Gayle was old European blood you know. So beautiful, like Allissa, and she didn't want her...soiled. Then when Gayle died..." He shrugged. "I was busy with my work. I had struggled up from nothing, you know. I wanted to buy her everything she wanted. Everything she needed."

"So you bought her a position at The Lone Oak Ranch, thinking that would be enough."

Vandegard scowled. "If it's more money you want—"

"Damn the money. And damn you!" Tyrel stormed.

Vandegard's brows rose under his hat, and then he chuckled.

"Why don't you take the money, Ty?" asked a soft voice. Tyrel swung about.

Hannah stood there, her expression fragile, her eyes wide.

"Or is it too much of a hardship putting up with me any longer?"

"Hannah." Her name slipped from him like a prayer.

"Allissa," Vandegard gasped. "Baby, don't get the wrong idea."

"The wrong idea?" Her tone was strained. She backed up a pace, her fists tight. "And what idea might that be, Daddy? That you lied to me? That you said my life was in danger? That you sent this two-bit actor to accost me in a parking lot? That you sent me away—made me fear for my life—for *your* life. And all the time you were paying Ty to keep me out of your hair. What? Were you afraid I might insult another of your friends?"

"Baby." Vandegard's long face had crumbled. "It's not like that." He stepped forward, holding out his hands in silent supplication. "Don't you see? I failed you. All those years I spent away—and your mother…" He paused. "I failed you, Allissa. I didn't want you to grow old without having a chance at what I had. A chance to do something you care passionately about."

She said nothing, but watched them all, her eyes cold chips of blue sapphire.

"You never had a chance to succeed, Allissa. Never had a chance to *try*. That's all I wanted for you. You have such life, such talent. But you were becoming…"

"An ice princess?" she supplied.

Vandegard shook his head. "My princess, yes. But never made of ice. I knew better. But others couldn't see it. And I was afraid that maybe you couldn't, either. Colonel Shelby told me long ago that I would spoil you. That I was ruining your heart."

She tilted her head slightly. "So you decided to give me heart by having me attacked?" She glared at Stone. He backed away a step, holding his offended arm. "By lying to me?"

"I—"

She cut him off with a harsh laugh. "And all the time I thought I was needed, thought I was doing something worthwhile." She flashed her gaze to Tyrel.

His heart stopped cold in his chest. "Hannah," he murmured.

"My name's *not* Hannah. It's Allissa! Allissa Clifton Vandegard! And you've known it all along."

"No." It was the only word he could find in his shattered world.

"No? But you knew I was rich—just a spoiled child whose own father couldn't bear to have her around. But you could put up with me—for enough money. Was it worth it, Tyrel? Did he pay you extra to sleep with me?"

He couldn't speak, couldn't move. The truth seemed a thousand miles away.

"You slept with her?" Vandegard's hand closed on Ty's arm, swinging him around.

Tyrel jerked out of his grasp. "Hannah," he said, but she was already running away.

"Damn you!" Vandegard stormed.

He was an old man, but he had fury behind his punch. Tyrel reeled sideways beneath the blow. Vandegard came on, large and incensed, but Ty ducked beneath his punch.

"Dammit!" he rasped, ducking again as his own pickup raced from the rodeo grounds. "She's leaving. For once in your life think of your daughter."

The fury went out of Vandegard like hot air from a balloon. "Dear God," he said, his face pale. "Where's she going?"

Ty watched her leave. "Anywhere we're not," he said softly.

THEY WERE THE WORST TWO weeks of Tyrel's life. The police found his pickup less than twenty miles from the rodeo grounds, parked in front of Duane's Café. But Hannah was nowhere to be found. He could only assume she had hitchhiked from there. But to where?

Under some duress, Vandegard had given him a list of phone numbers where she might be found. Ty had called each one. No answer. He'd then telephoned every acquaintance she'd ever known. Still nothing.

It was finally dumb luck that helped him find her—old men in overalls, talking over coffee.

Raymond Caliber had hired himself a new hand, one of them had said. A woman! A looker she was. Could sit a horse like a centaur.

And so it was that Tyrel stood in someone else's barn on the southern border of North Dakota. Inside the arena, Hannah-Allissa rode a liver chestnut in tight circles.

Tyrel leaned up against the wall and watched her, feeling his heart slap against his ribs and his muscles finally relax one by one. For the first time in weeks, he could breathe without feeling as if his chest were bound in barbed wire.

She was safe. She was well. That would have to be enough for him—at least for now.

"You always had a damn fine seat," he said quietly.

She jerked toward him at the sound of his voice. He watched her face go pale. The chestnut faltered. Hannah tightened her grip on the reins and pushed the gelding on. Except for the sound of the horse's hoofbeats, the whole world seemed silent.

"How did you find me?" she asked.

Two weeks of sleeplessness, endless phone calls, hopeless leads, dogged badgering, relentless prayer. Even now, his knees felt weak, but whether it was fatigue or the sight of her, he wasn't sure.

"A woman like you is bound to attract attention, Hannah. I asked around."

"I assume Daddy is paying you well for your time," she said.

He straightened from the wall. Regardless of his fears, neither his nor her father's stupidity had broken her spirit. The muscles in the back of his neck relaxed a tad.

"I never knew who you were, Hannah. Not until a couple of weeks ago when I talked to your dad."

"Of course you saw no reason to inform me of your correspondence with him. Even though..." Her voice cracked. She scowled and went on. "Even though we had become...intimate by then."

He watched her. She was all wounded pride and elegant toughness. It was little wonder his heart would never recover. "I think you've kept a couple of things from me, too, Hannah."

She didn't look at him, but her brow remained furrowed. "He was paying you, wasn't he? All the time I thought I was achieving something on my own. Earning your respect. He was paying you."

The gelding's hoofbeats seemed to echo the beat of Tyrel's heart.

"You always had my respect. Ever since I saw you trekking through the snow in nothing but a towel and a glare."

"You were being compensated to keep me," she said. "Paid—like I was some kid sent off to summer camp."

"I never thought of you as a kid."

"You must have laughed. I didn't know how to feed a calf. Didn't know how to cinch a saddle."

Okay. He'd laughed. But the memories of those past moments were like sunshine on his soul now. And if the truth be known, she'd gotten her licks in. "Well...you can be an infuriating woman."

"You made fun of my roping skills."

"You insulted my ranch."

"You insulted my accent."

"You insulted my whole family."

"You made a bet about me—like I was a...a racehorse or something."

"You threw milk in my face."

"You worked me like a dog."

"You set fire to my kitchen, turned my ranch upside down and broke my brother's leg."

She came back with no rebuttals, but let the gelding carry her in yet another circle.

"It must have been hard—putting up with me."

He watched her—the way she held her hands just so, the way she hugged the chestnut's sides, the way her mouth pursed in that odd combination of fragility and toughness. His heart contracted.

"Yeah, it was hard," he said. "Damn hard, but what can I do? I'm in love with you."

The reins fell from Hannah's hands. The gelding shuffled to a halt.

Her face went absolutely pale, but she gathered her composure with the same aplomb that she gathered the reins—swiftly, unerringly. "What's Daddy paying you to say that?"

"Damn the money!" He all but yelled the words, losing his composure just as quickly as she'd gained hers. "And damn your father! It's not my fault he didn't know what he had in you. I know! I see!" He paused, breathing hard. "And I love you."

She blinked her eyes. They were unearthly bright, but she shook her head, denying her tears just as she denied his words. "I don't believe you, Tyrel."

He narrowed his eyes and paced across the arena. "You do believe me," he growled, staring up at her. "And that scares you."

"Scares *me!*"

"Scares the hell out of you. Because for the first time in your life someone knows who you really are."

"Really? And who am I?" she shouted.

Silence settled slowly in.

"You're Hannah Nelson," he said into the quiet.

She stared at him, then finally shook her head. "I'm not. Not even if I wanted to be. I'm Allissa Clifton Vandegard."

Silence.

"Then I want to marry *her*," Ty said.

Her eyes went wide and her lips parted in surprise, but in a moment she drew herself up straight, though her hands shook on the reins.

"A rich daddy can convince—"

He cut her short. "I don't want to hear your sorry excuses, Hannah. Do whatever you have to do. Get me prenuptial papers. I'll sign them. Hell, I'll have them drawn up myself."

The arena echoed with silence.

"You don't even have to live with me," he said, his voice going soft. "I'll take whatever I can get. One day a month. One night a year. Live in New York if you must. LA. Wherever you—"

"Is that what you think I want?" she asked, her voice cracking. "You think I want to live in LA?"

"I don't know what the hell you want!" he yelled.

"Then you don't know me very well," she yelled back.

He clenched his fists, drew a deep breath, and forced himself to relax. "I want to know you, Hannah," he said softly. "I want to dedicate my life to knowing you."

For a moment all the world was still, then she said, "And I want you," she whispered, and slipped from the saddle into his arms.

"Hannah!" He squeezed her to him, feeling that his heart would burst. "I'm sorry. I should have—"

"Shh." She laughed, then kissed him and laughed again. "You can make it up to me."

He kissed her back—his heart full, his dreams complete. She was his, forever and always. But her words niggled at his mind. He pushed her slowly to arm's length. "Make it up to you?" he asked suspiciously.

"Sure. Sing me a song at the next rodeo and I'll marry you," she said, and slipping her hand behind his neck, she kissed him again.

Head Down Under for twelve tales of heated romance in beautiful and untamed Australia!

Here's a sneak preview of the first novel in THE AUSTRALIANS

Outback Heat **by Emma Darcy available July 1998**

'HAVE I DONE something wrong?' Angie persisted, wishing Taylor would emit a sense of camaraderie instead of holding an impenetrable reserve.

'Not at all,' he assured her. 'I would say a lot of things right. You seem to be fitting into our little Outback community very well. I've heard only good things about you.'

'They're nice people,' she said sincerely. Only the Maguire family kept her shut out of their hearts.

'Yes,' he agreed. 'Though I appreciate it's taken considerable effort from you. It is a world away from what you're used to.'

The control Angie had been exerting over her feelings snapped. He wasn't as blatant as his aunt in his prejudice against her but she'd felt it coming through every word he'd spoken and she didn't deserve any of it.

'Don't judge me by your wife!'

His jaw jerked. A flicker of some dark emotion destroyed the steady power of his probing gaze.

'No two people are the same. If you don't know that, you're a man of very limited vision. So I come from the city as your wife did! That doesn't stop me from being an individual in my own right.'

She straightened up, proudly defiant, furiously angry with the situation. 'I'm *me*. Angie Cordell. And it's time you took the blinkers off your eyes, Taylor Maguire.'

Then she whirled away from him, too agitated by the explosive expulsion of her emotion to keep facing him.

The storm outside hadn't yet eased. There was nowhere to go. She stopped at the window, staring blindly at the torrential rain. The thundering on the roof was almost deafening but it wasn't as loud as the silence behind her.

'You want me to go, don't you? You've given me a month's respite and now you want me to leave and channel my energies somewhere else.'

'I didn't say that, Angie.'

'You were working your way around it.' Bitterness at his tactics spewed the suspicion. 'Do you have your first choice of governess waiting in the wings?'

'No. I said I'd give you a chance.'

'Have you?' She swung around to face him. 'Have you really, Taylor?'

He hadn't moved. He didn't move now except to make a gesture of appeasement. 'Angie, I was merely trying to ascertain how you felt.'

'Then let me tell you your cynicism was shining through every word.'

He frowned, shook his head. 'I didn't mean to hurt you.' The blue eyes fastened on hers with devastating sincerity. 'I truly did not come in here to take you down or suggest you leave.'

Her heart jiggled painfully. He might be speaking the truth but the judgements were still there, the judgements that ruled his attitude towards her, that kept her shut out of his life, denied any real sharing with him, denied his confidence and trust. She didn't know why it meant so much to her but it did. It did. And the need to fight for justice from him was as much a raging torrent inside her as the rain outside.

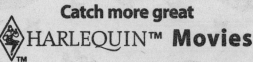

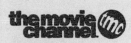 

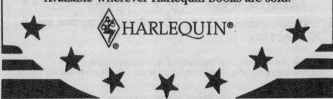

LOVE & LAUGH

INTO AUGUST!

#49 REGARDING RITA
Gwen Pemberton

Waitress Rita Lynn is pregnant and her almost-fiancé is out of the country—out of her life, truth be told. Enter widower Nate Morrow, a city-wearied divorce lawyer who thinks he's going to find peace and simplicity in small-town life. Hah! Not in Hooperville, not when every matchmaker in town—which is everyone—thinks he's the answer to the problem "regarding Rita."

#50 GETTIN' LUCKY
Kimberly Raye

Lucky Myers was really *un*lucky in love. So, when she came across a gorgeous cowboy swimming in the buff, she didn't know what to do—run or enjoy the show. And when he asked her to spend time on his ranch, she was floored! That is, until the sexy cowpoke asked her to be his *nanny!*

LOVE & LAUGHTER™